The Final Squeeze . . .

From behind a panel of mirrors, a figure moved. The king of the Maya was alone, and his heavy, even breathing filled the empty room. The man behind the mirror was dressed in a beggar's rags, but on his neck hung the precious topaz amulet of the high priest of the Olmec. He moved slowly, quietly as a cat, to the king's throne. Then, with practiced fingers, he encircled the old man's neck and squeezed. The king's eyes opened in silent terror.

"I have waited ten years to find the magic spears of fire," the priest whispered, staring directly into the king's face. "And now you have shown them to me. The Olmec will kill your people, destroy your gods, and level your kingdom to ashes. When you are gone, there will be nothing left of you but your rotting bones."

The king opened his mouth in a futile gesture. No sound came out. His face started to shake with spasms; his eyes bulged. He reached up with one trembling hand and clasped the topaz amulet, cold against his hot, numbing skin.

"Look in my eyes, old man, and despair," the priest whispered as he choked the life out of the dying king.

THE DESTROYER SERIES:

#1 CREATED, THE DESTROYER
#2 DEATH CHECK
#3 CHINESE PUZZLE
#4 MAFIA FIX
#5 DR. QUAKE
#6 DEATH THERAPY
#7 UNION BUST
#8 SUMMIT CHASE
#9 MURDERER'S SHIELD
#10 TERROR SQUAD
#11 KILL OR CURE
#12 SLAVE SAFARI
#13 ACID ROCK
#14 JUDGMENT DAY
#15 MURDER WARD
#16 OIL SLICK
#17 LAST WAR DANCE
#18 FUNNY MONEY
#19 HOLY TERROR
#20 ASSASSIN'S PLAY-OFF
#21 DEADLY SEEDS
#22 BRAIN DRAIN
#23 CHILD'S PLAY
#24 KING'S CURSE
#25 SWEET DREAMS
#26 IN ENEMY HANDS
#27 THE LAST TEMPLE
#28 SHIP OF DEATH
#29 THE FINAL DEATH
#30 MUGGER BLOOD
#31 THE HEAD MEN
#32 KILLER CHROMOSOMES
#33 VOODOO DIE
#34 CHAINED REACTION
#35 LAST CALL
#36 POWER PLAY
#37 BOTTOM LINE
#38 BAY CITY BLAST
#39 MISSING LINK
#40 DANGEROUS GAMES
#41 FIRING LINE
#42 TIMBER LINE
#43 MIDNIGHT MAN
#44 BALANCE OF POWER
#45 SPOILS OF WAR
#46 NEXT OF KIN
#47 DYING SPACE
#48 PROFIT MOTIVE
#49 SKIN DEEP
#50 KILLING TIME
#51 SHOCK VALUE
#52 FOOL'S GOLD

ATTENTION: SCHOOLS AND CORPORATIONS

PINNACLE Books are available at quantity discounts with bulk purchases for educational, business or special promotional use. For further details, please write to: SPECIAL SALES MANAGER, Pinnacle Books, Inc., 1430 Broadway, New York, NY 10018.

WRITE FOR OUR FREE CATALOG

If there is a Pinnacle Book you want—and you cannot find it locally—it is available from us simply by sending the title and price plus 75¢ to cover mailing and handling costs to:

Pinnacle Books, Inc.
Reader Service Department
1430 Broadway
New York, NY 10018

Please allow 6 weeks for delivery.

———Check here if you want to receive our catalog regularly.

TIME TRIAL

PINNACLE BOOKS NEW YORK

This is a work of fiction. All the characters and events portrayed in this book are fictional, and any resemblance to real people or incidents is purely coincidental.

Destroyer #53: Time Trial

Copyright © 1983 by Richard Sapir and Warren Murphy

All rights reserved, including the right to reproduce this book or portions thereof in any form.

An original Pinnacle Book edition, published for the first time anywhere.

First printing, August 1983

ISBN: 0-523-41563-X

Cover illustration by Hector Garrido

Printed in the United States of America

PINNACLE BOOKS, INC.
1430 Broadway
New York, New York 10018

A Dedication:

For Kathy Rook, whose stories are wonderful; for Archie Edward Hinson, $2 worth; and for the Princeton Karate Club 'cause Megan said so.
—Warren Murphy

And an Interruption:

Hold! What are these idiotic inscriptions? Who are these people? I, Chiun, now dedicate this book properly. For Don Davisson and Sally Vogel who are disgusted with all of you and the way you have ignored me for years and who have now formed The House of Sinanju Tribute Society, Post Office Box 17593, Portland, Oregon 97217. This is a good thing and I, the Master of Sinanju, approve.
—Chiun

CHAPTER ONE

The priest led the procession through the cave of Puch, god of the Underworld. Past the six snarling heads of felled jaguars in the Hall of Balam they came, the holy men who chanted, holding aloft the dead sacrificed birds. Warriors walked behind them, chieftains gathered from distant jungle tribes.

They were Olmec, each marked by a black spot of ash on his forehead. They moved slowly, in secrecy, because that was the way of the Olmec. Secrecy brought power, and so they walked softly into the Inner Chambers, where the magic would take place.

Past the stone sentry of a man bearing an ape's head they came, past the Wall of Days, where garishly colored paintings depicted the Olmec's enemies in obscene postures, then past the demonic likeness of Puch himself, Master of the Dead, tangled snakes emanating from his ears, his luminescent jade eyes glowing.

Ahead of them all walked the high priest, the *h'men* or visionary, he of the Sight. Festooned in spotted cat skins, his hair matted and stinking of blood from the birds sacrificed in the way of his people, he prepared for the ceremony to come, pulling his strength inward, blocking out his senses until he could hear only the heavy thrum of his own heartbeat, accentuated with every pace by the movement of the amber amulet he wore around his neck.

The amulet was a talisman, believed by the Olmec to bring on visions of the future that only the ordained high priests of their tribe could see. But the priest himself knew the stone to be worthless.

He had possessed the Sight since he was a child. The priests who had worn the amulet then, had known nothing of what was to come to their people, but even as a child he had known. In his visions, he knew that what was to come was no less than the curse of Puch himself.

Death. Death for all of them. Death for ages, forever. He had known it then, but no one had listened. Now the elder priests were dead, killed by their own people, and the young *h'men* had risen to wear the amulet of leadership. If he had failed, he, too, would have died.

But he did not fail, and what lay in the innermost chamber of the cave proved his victory. His vision had foreseen that the gods would come to rule the Olmec's enemies in the kingdom on the other side of the fire mountain Bocatan, and that those enemies would prevail.

The visions were true; they were always true. The strange gods in their flying sky-chariot had come to aid the Olmec's enemies with weapons wrought from shafts of lightning, which they held in their bare hands. The Olmec had been driven away, forbidden to walk above ground.

But even the gods can be challenged. And if they are conquered, the future can be changed. The Olmec had both challenged and conquered the enemy gods, who lay now, captured, defeated, inside the inner chamber of the cave, their hands and legs bound like those of ordinary mortals, their throats parched, the taste of fear in their mouths. The gods waited to die.

The entourage halted at the entrance to the chamber as five of the warriors rolled away the great stone that served as a door. Inside, the holy men placed the dead birds at the feet of the stone likeness of Puch, which dominated the cold room. Demonic-looking obsidian snakes guarded the chamber from the curse of light. The high priest stepped forward.

"Hear me, O Dread One," he intoned, raising his arms high. "For you have we defied the prophecies. For you have we seized the enemy gods. For you do we make sacrifice of them."

He lowered his arms and turned to face the altar across the chamber. Six stone slabs stretched across the length of the room. On top of each was one of the fallen deities, bound and helpless. They craned their necks to watch the priest as he prepared to come to them.

From the clothes they wore, each of the holy

men took the snow-white spine of a sting ray and placed it at the priest's feet. Kneeling, the priest picked them up and pierced his flesh with them: his arms, his chest, belly, thighs, and hands. The darts were painful; they ripped the flesh where they struck and caused the priest's blood to fall in heavy droplets to the ground, but the priest's face remained expressionless. Ahead of him lay the bed of burning coals to be used in his final purification. Smoke rose from it like steam.

He stood, hearing his heart beat slower and deeper, as the blood falling around his feet became a pool of red, his body streaked. He would feel no pain now. The moment had come. He walked forward.

The burning coals bit into his bare feet like hungry animals, crumbling beneath his weight. Blood coursing down his arms mingled with the sweat of pain and heat and dripped off his fingers to sizzle on the steaming, spitting coals. He was the *h'men*, he of the Sight; in his hands lay the future of his people. He moved silently, steadily, leaving a trail of burning blood behind.

The enemy gods watched. They were amazed, their alien features twisted. All but the leader. He watched, too, but his face was different. It held a look of serene detachment, even of excitement. This god, possibly because he was a god, was not afraid to die. When the high priest stepped off the coals to stand directly before them, the gods began to babble in fear. One cried out. Another wept when the priest removed the great carved obsidian dagger from his belt and walked behind them, into position. Only the leader-god's face remained impassive. He spoke something in his strange tongue, and the weeping god became silent. As the priest held the dagger high above the leader-god's head, the others chanted a strange prayer in unison. The leader did not join them.

He watched the priest. For a moment, the priest was distracted by the god's strange eyes. They were clouded, as if behind them were a deep mist, but unafraid. The priest respected this god, even if he was not of the Olmec. When the ceremony was over, he would command that the bodies of the others be given to the fire mountain Bocatan as offering. But the leader's would remain here, where his spirit would serve Puch. This one was worthy of Puch.

"Dread One, I commend them to you," the priest said. Then, with one powerful downward thrust, he plunged the dagger into the forehead of the leader-god. Blood spurted out of him, streaming over the silver garment he wore, cloth that felt wet to the touch, even when dry. Now the blood ran off the strange clothing as if it were running off a bank of clay. The god's world, the priest thought, must be a strange place indeed.

The others shrieked like cowards. They were the lesser gods, unworthy. The priest finished them off quickly, lodging the dagger where he could. When he was finished, his arms were covered with blood and bone.

"Begone with them," the priest said with

contempt. "But the king god stays here. Bring wine and bread for his sustenance in the Land of the Dead."

When the work was finished and the priest stood over the dead gods, his arms spattered, he listened to himself. The breath rushed heavily out of him, and his heart was still thudding with the kill. The muscles in his arms twitched. His fingers felt weak. The gods had given him the Sight, but he was not a peaceful visionary. The excitement of the kill instilled a feeling in him close to lust. There would never be a woman for him, he knew, because no woman could satisfy him as well as death in the moment he inflicted it. The first sharp thrust into a man's living body, stilling it forever, brought him more pleasure than a thousand courtesans.

Exercising all the control he could will, he placed the stone dagger carefully in its sheath on the column beside the slabs holding the bodies.

His head ached. A refrain, feeling like a black thread in his brain, began to voice itself, intruding and unwelcome.

The weapons. The shafts of fire.

The gods had been captured without the magic weapons that had driven the Olmec into defeat. Without them, victory would always belong to the favorites of the alien gods, to those who dwelled in the kingdom on the other side of the fire mountain Bocatan.

The priest's task was not yet finished. Before his people could come to power, he would have to steal the fire of the gods.

Unnerved after his ordeal, controlling each small step, the priest walked up the thirty-three steps out of the cave. Outside, rising above the cave, roared the waterfall that hid the shrine from view of the Olmec's enemies. The priest stripped himself beside the thundering waters, wincing as he pulled the white ray spines from his body. Then, his wounds bleeding freely, he stepped into the cold water to cleanse himself.

He washed the blood from his hair and hands—his own, the sacrificed birds', the blood of the alien gods from their distant world. They were all one in the water, as the Olmec believed past and future to be one.

Past and future. The priest would change the future and thus alter the past for all the ages of man to come. He had stilled the voice of the gods. The prophecy would not come to pass. And now he would find the gods' weapons and with them lead the Olmec to eternal triumph.

He rose from the water and looked toward Bocatan. The fire mountain was sleeping now, as it had slept for a hundred years, its burning orange floods contained within it. Beyond it lay Yaxbenhaltun, the vast kingdom of the enemy, the kingdom prophesied to rule over the entire world, causing all others to perish in its wake.

The kingdom of the Maya.

The priest looked back once on the poison fields that surrounded the Olmec camp. Their legacy of death. Then, naked, he walked toward the enemy kingdom beyond the mountain.

CHAPTER TWO

His name was Remo and he was squeezing water from a stone—or trying to. A four-foot-high mound of fine sand stood beside him in silent testimony to his failure. Since before midnight he had been collecting rocks off the stony floor of the Mojave desert, handling each to test for shape and weight, pressing, concentrating the pressure evenly over every part of his hand so that the rock imploded, giving up what moisture it had.

Except that the rocks in this desert held no moisture. It was August, and even the first breaking rays of sun in the red-dawned morning were hot enough to redden the skin of a normal white man.

Not that Remo was normal. An entire government organization had been devised to make Remo as abnormal as possible. The organization, CURE, had taken a young policeman, framed him for a crime he didn't commit, sentenced him to die in an electric chair that didn't work, declared him dead to the world, then set about retraining his muscles and nerves and mind so that Remo was, in his own body, the most effective fighting machine in the employ of the government of the United States.

CURE's director, Harold W. Smith, founded the organization long ago as a deterrent against crime, at the direction of a man who was then President of the United States. But unlike other law enforcement agencies, CURE worked. It worked because it operated against the law. Outside the Constitution. There was nothing legal about CURE. Smith's own base of operations, a powerful bank of computers inside the executive offices of Folcroft Sanitarium in Rye, New York, and duplicated in another bank on the island of St. Maarten, regularly tapped other information centers, paid informants, instigated IRS investigations, forged documents, blackmailed politicians, circulated rumors, and generally did whatever Smith deemed necessary to halt the activities of those criminals who were normally beyond the pale of the law. And then there was Remo, the enforcement arm of CURE. Remo was probably the single most illegal individual in the world, let alone the U.S. government.

Remo was an assassin. His job was to kill people—with his hands, his feet, his wrists, his shoulders, even his neck. He killed efficiently, exquisitely, and, most of the time, uncomplainingly. No government could ask for better.

The President of the United States, the one person besides Harold Smith and Remo himself who knew of CURE's existence, referred to Remo only as "that special person." But in the president's mind, as in the mind of every president before him who knew about CURE, Remo was no person. He was a tool, a killing machine, and the main reason why CURE had to remain the best-kept secret in the country.

Smith had selected Remo for CURE, but he had not trained him. No American in history had ever learned to kill the way Remo could kill. For Remo's extraordinary instruction, Smith had turned to the East, to a small village in North Korea, which had been producing assassins for hire since before the writing of history. In the village of Sinanju, one man existed who knew the secrets of the sun source of the martial arts—an eighty-year-old man who could create a killing machine from a dead man. His name was Chiun, Master of Sinanju, whose job it was to see to it that Remo was never normal again.

Through the years, Remo's body had changed, his digestive system simplified, his nervous system rendered more sensitive and complex than other humans'. But his mind had changed, too, adapted to the ways of his ancient master, so that Remo now was less a tool of the government than he was heir to the ancient House of Sinanju.

And so instead of killing people for the U.S. government, Remo was standing in the middle of the desert squeezing rocks for Chiun.

"Again," the old man said with exaggerated patience, the white wisps of hair on his head and chin sparkling in the spectacularly bright sunlight.

"There's no water in these rocks, Little Father," Remo groused. "From the looks of this place, there hasn't been water here since the dinosaurs. Where are we, anyway?"

They had come to this place via the northern route, meaning by way of the North Pole. Every six months Chiun led Remo on a training expedition into extremes of climate, where he would observe his protégé as Remo performed tasks so difficult that they were likely never to arise in the line of duty. He grilled Remo in mountain running, tree splitting, swimming beneath twenty-foot arctic ice floes, and now, for reasons obscure to Remo, he felt it necessary to watch his pupil extract water from a rock.

"It is unimportant where we are. The terrain is acceptable. That is all that matters. Again, Remo." He tossed Remo another rock.

"Meaning we're lost," Remo said, crumbling the rock to dust.

Chiun shrugged. "What does it matter? If one is not in Sinanju, it makes no difference where one is."

"It does if you're in the middle of the Gobi desert."

Chiun clucked. "The Gobi. Only a white man would take this for the Gobi. Have you taken no notice of the flora?" He pointed to a patch of white near the eastern horizon.

"That's not flora," Remo said. "It's the bones of some poor sucker caught out here after seven A.M. That's fauna. Dead fauna."

"Complaints, complaints." The old Oriental adjusted his crimson satin robe and tossed Remo another rock.

"How long do I have to keep doing this?"

"You do not have to keep doing anything. Just do it once. Then we may progress."

"Progress where?"

"To the jungle, I think. You could use more jungle experience."

"Oh, great. Just great. I suppose you'll want me to squeeze rocks in the jungle, too."

"Don't be foolish. Anyone can get water from a rock in a jungle."

"Yeah, I know. It takes imagination to get water from a rock in the desert."

"It is not a matter of imagination," Chiun snapped. "It is a matter of timing. Hold the rock downward, so that the moisture cannot evaporate before you see it." He demonstrated.

Remo held out his hand, imitating the old man, weighing the rock between his fingers. "Like this?"

"Yes," Chiun said crisply. "Of course, it is no good now that I've had to tell you."

"Hey, it's working." Remo felt the faint accumulation of moisture on his skin. He opened his hand, and the dry dust blew away in the wind. He rubbed his fingers together.

"This isn't water," he said.

"Oh? And what is it, o knowledgeable one? Camel dung?"

He sniffed his fingers. "It's oil."

"Oil? Desert oil?" His eyes glinted. "Worth many millions in gold?"

"Motor oil," Remo said.

"Oh," Chiun said, his interest evaporated.

"Say, I know where we are. It's California, right?"

"All barbarian places look the same to me."

"It's got to be California. We've been heading west, we haven't crossed any oceans, and I saw a sign for Nevada two days ago."

"We could be in U-Haul," Chiun said loftily.

"That's Utah, and we're not there."

"How do you know?"

Just then a sound like an atomic blast roared behind them and spread to crack the air all around them.

"Because of that," Remo said. He searched the sky. After a moment, he pointed upward, squinting. "Look there." High overhead, standing out against the blue sky, was a small black object. It rose in a wake of deafening noise until it disappeared. "We're near Edwards Air Force Base," Remo said. "They test experimental aircraft here. See? That must be one of them."

"One of many unsuccessful experiments, I imagine," Chiun sniffed. He had ridden in experimental government aircraft. As far as he was concerned, no vehicle that did not offer feature-length movies was worth its tailwind.

"You don't mean unsuccessful, Little Father. You mean unenjoyable."

"I do not mean unsuccessful?"

"No," Remo said.

"Then why is that machine falling?"

The black speck appeared to be growing larger. There was no sound.

"Maybe they turned the engines off," Remo offered. As the object tumbled downward, it began to take on a shape—angular, with projectiles, and two flat, triangular wings spinning in a corkscrew as the craft raced toward earth.

Another object, much smaller, popped out of the plummeting aircraft and continued its own descent parallel to the plane's.

"The pilot," Remo said. "He's bailing out." A thin stream of what looked like fluid snaked out of the pilot's back and streamed above him for long seconds as the man fell.

"Open it," Remo shouted. "Open the parachute!"

"He may have thought of that himself," Chiun said dryly.

"He's got a streamer," Remo whispered. Then, in a flash of light and sound, the plane exploded in midair, the shock waves sending the falling pilot hurtling through the sky, his suit in flames.

Remo ran instinctively with the man, following his crazy trajectory. The pilot was close enough to hear now. He had removed his helmet and was screaming. He was falling end over end, the flames lapping at his legs, his hands shielding his face from the fire he was unable to control.

"Find your center," Chiun said quietly, stepping aside. His criticism of Remo was for practice, for the endless exercises Remo was expected to perform. If he did them perfectly, Chiun still found something to criticize because perfection did not grow from praise. And perfection one time was not enough. Through the years of Remo's arduous training, the old man had made him repeat the exercises again and again, until they were perfect, after they were perfect, and after they had been perfect every time, because he knew that when it became necessary for Remo to use his skills, perfection was required. The first time.

Remo was balanced on the balls of his feet, shifting his weight as his eyes followed the falling body. Then, when the burning pilot was a hundred feet above ground, Remo closed his eyes.

Chiun had taught him that the way of Sinanju was to make one's body one with its surroundings, to feel the space around objects rather than see those objects. It was how the Masters of Sinanju had been able to move, silently, through the ages of man's civilization, without disturbing even the dry leaves beneath their feet, and how they controlled their senses and involuntary functions. They *were* their environment.

And now Remo, behind his eyes, became the air parting for the panicked figure that fell through it, became the fire on the man's clothes, became the man himself, with his jerking muscles and the terror that tore through him, making his balance erratic. Remo was all of these things, and so when he began his slow, crouching spin upward, preparing for the spring that would propel him off the ground and bring him back again, his eyes were closed, his muscles relaxed, his mind unthinking, fully concentrating, open yet filled. He sprang out of the coil in perfect balance, seeming to lift off the ground. Then, just before the pilot would have smashed to earth, Remo encircled him with both arms and carried him in the spin downward with him, breaking the momentum of the fall. He settled softly on the sandy ground, leaving only two circles where his feet had touched.

Chiun was with him at the moment when he set the pilot down, tearing off the man's burning clothes with one swift incision from the fingernail of his index finger. In less than a second the fire was out and the man lay on the ground. His skin was reddened but not charred, and no bones were broken.

"I—I can't believe it," the pilot said.

"Don't. You never saw us, okay? Let's get out of here," Remo said to Chiun.

"But you saved my life."

"Okay. So now you can save mine. Just keep quiet about this."

The pilot looked over the two strange men. One was an Oriental in full regalia. He was less than five feet tall and looked a hundred years old. The other was a good-looking young white man in a T-shirt. Nothing exceptional about him except for his wrists, which were unusually thick.

"You two on the run from the law or something?"

Remo winked and made a show of picking his teeth.

The pilot smiled. "Well, I don't know what your secret is, but it's safe with me. Thanks a million. My wife's in the hospital having a kid today. I don't know what she would do if I bought the old farm now. She promised me a boy."

In the distance, they heard the approaching sirens of a rescue squad. "Good for you, champ," Remo said, patting the pilot gently on the shoulder. "Have a good life."

"Hey, wait . . ." The pilot pressed himself onto his elbows to see behind him. The old man and the guy with the thick wrists were already nearly out of sight.

"I suppose you know where you're going?" Chiun asked.

Remo nodded. "Following my nose."

"My nose senses nothing but the repugnant odor of chickens boiled in oil," Chiun said distastefully.

"Bingo. A fried chicken joint. That means a town. Motels are in towns. That's where we're going."

"We were progressing toward the jungle," Chiun said.

"I've been in a jungle. You know what they say about jungles. You see one, you seen 'em all.

Besides, I've got to call Smitty. I haven't talked to him in four days."

"Surely the Emperor Smith understands that his assassins must practice their art."

"The Emperor Smith understands that I work for him. C'mon, Chiun. We could use a night in a motel. This Boy Scout stuff is getting old fast."

"It is you who are getting old. Old white flesh, as toneless as the underside of an octopus. This is the legacy of your race."

"You can have the vibrating bed."

The old man's almond eyes turned into shrewd little slits. "And cable television."

"You've got it."

"Also the bathtub. I will use the bathtub first."

Remo sighed. "All right."

"And room service. It is too much to ask one of my years to walk to his food."

"I thought you were planning to walk us both to the jungle."

"This is different. The stench of fried animals saps my strength."

"I don't think motels have room service."

Chiun stopped short. "I will not go unless I can have room service."

"All right, already," Remo said. "We'll get room service."

Twenty minutes later, Chiun was lying on the vibrating bed, chuckling and singing tuneless Korean songs as the television blared at full volume and the motel reservations clerk plopped down two paper containers of plain rice and two glasses of water, for which Remo had paid him fifty dollars.

"That it, mister?" the clerk said.

Remo nodded, sticking his finger in his ear to block out the noise. He had dialed Smith's number at Folcroft directly, without going through the obscure telephone routings that Remo couldn't remember, and that meant he would have to speak to Smith in code, which he also couldn't remember. Something about Aunt Mildred. Aunt Mildred always figured into Smith's calls. Aunt Mildred doing something meant that Smith was to return the call within three minutes, to California. That would be the right one, but what she was doing was the code. "Washing" meant Remo needed money; no point in that one. "Aunt Mildred is gone" meant the mission was accomplished. But California . . .

"Yes?" Smith's lemony voice twanged on the other end of the line.

"Uh . . ."

"I beg your pardon?"

"Aunt Mildred picks her nose," Remo said winsomely. "In California."

Smith sighed. "I've been waiting for you. Keep the line open for three minutes so I can trace this call, then wait. I'll come to you."

He arrived within twenty minutes.

"That was fast," Remo said.

"I wasn't at Folcroft." Smith settled down his straw fedora. He wore a three-piece suit, even though it was ninety degrees outside. "I was at an investigation that you should have been conducting." He looked testily to Remo. "Since you couldn't be reached, I had to make the preliminary inquiries myself."

"I'm sure you made a fine assassin, Emperor," Chiun said fawningly.

Smith gave an exasperated snort. "I an not an emperor, Chiun," he explained for the hundredth time. "This is a free country. A democracy. In a democracy—"

Chiun was nodding and smiling broadly. "Never mind," Smith said, directing his attention back to Remo. "As a matter of fact, I was quite nearby, at the UCLA Medical Center. Your call was routed automatically to the telephone in my briefcase. While you've been vacationing, the university and the federal government have been in an uproar."

"Some vacation," Remo said glumly. "Feeling up rocks."

"Well, whatever you've been doing, I'm afraid I've got to cut it short. There's something you have to attend to." He fumbled in his briefcase.

"What a shame," Remo said, smiling. "Just when I was beginning to look forward to seeing the jungle." Chiun stared at him blackly.

"You were?" Smith looked up from his briefcase. He held a sheet of white paper in his hand.

"Sure. I love the jungle. All those neat flies and poisonous snakes. Nothing like it. But duty calls, right, Smitty?"

"Er—yes." He handed Remo the paper. On it was a hand-drawn map.

Remo looked at it from several different angles. "Where's this?"

Smith smiled faintly, the expression looking peculiar and uncomfortable on his face. "The Peten jungle of Guatemala. Quite a coincidence. You won't be disappointed, after all."

"Thrilled," Remo said, ignoring Chiun's smug look. "Thrilled to death."

"It marks the location of an archaeological dig begun several months ago, sponsored by the University of California. There it is," he said, pointing to the map. "About fifty miles west of Progresso, south of the Ucimacita River. The archaelogists believed they'd found the remains of an ancient Mayan temple, which the locals call the Temple of Magic.

"Shortly after they excavated the site, though, a series of small earthquakes began disturbing the region. This, I understand, is part of the normal twenty-year cycle. The quakes weren't serious, but the archaeologists were afraid that some of the material they found in the temple would be damaged unless they could catalog it and clear it out quickly. Also, of course, the possibility of a big earthquake made them nervous. They wrote to the university requesting a second relief team to assist them, and sent along some samples of what they'd already excavated.

"What'd they find?"

"The usual. Pottery, that sort of thing. But quite old. The material was carbon tested at the university. It seems the samples they sent were made more than five thousand years ago."

"An upstart temple," Chiun said, yawning. "Probably a hippo cult."

"Hippo?" said Smith.

"He means hippie," Remo said.

"Oh. Listen to this," Smith said. He pulled out another sheet of paper from his briefcase. "It's a copy of the letter the archaeologists sent to the university." Holding the letter at arm's length, he read: "There is something else here—something that is without doubt the greatest find of this or any other century. I dare reveal no more until our evidence can be documented properly. But the possibility that this discovery may be destroyed utterly by earthquake or other natural causes cannot be borne. We urge you to relay our request for assistance to Doctors Diehl and Drake immediately."

"So who's Diehl and Drake?"

"Richard Diehl and Elizabeth Drake, the two most prominent archaeologists at the university. Both have written seminal works about the Mayan civilization. When they saw the material the expedition team sent, they left for the site right away."

"Think you could get to the point?" Remo asked wearily.

"The point is, when Diehl and Drake arrived, every member of the first archaeological team had been murdered."

"By rival archaeologists?"

"That was Diehl's first guess. From the mysterious letter the first team sent, he figured that they'd discovered something really rare—rare enough that someone else would kill them for it. But then, shortly after they arrived, Diehl and Drake themselves were ambushed." He paused, looking embarrassed.

"And?"

"I should explain first that I've just come from seeing Diehl. He's in the hospital, being treated for shock and exhaustion, and not quite coherent. He was the only one to survive the expedition."

"What's he sayng? That he was attacked by little men from Mars?"

"Not far from it, actually. He claims that the men who attacked the second expedition were definitely Indians of the variety found in Central America. Where his story gets hard to swallow is in the matter of weapons."

"Some Indian weapons are quite unusual," Chiun offered helpfully. "Curare-tipped spears, ropes weighted by knotted stones . . ."

"He claims they were carrying laser weapons," Smith said, flushing slightly.

Remo's eyebrows arched amusement. "Lasers? What were these guys carrying in their canteens?"

"If Dr. Diehl weren't the respected scholar he is, his observations would be dismissed out of hand," Smith said. "But he seems to be lucid on every point. He says that during the ambush, an earthquake of some magnitude occurred, trapping his associate, Dr. Drake, and some of the attackers. He used the opportunity to escape. He claims to be the only member of the team who wasn't killed.

"At Progresso, the town nearest the site, he notified the Red Cross. They sent a rescue helicopter. The helicopter sent one transmission, acknowledging that the rescue team had located the site, and then the transmission became garbled. The radio man on duty thinks the transmission included something about "exotic weapons." At any rate, Diehl swears that the Indians used lasers. His descriptions of the sound and sight of the weapons in operation vaguely resemble test data gathered by the military on laser weaponry, although we don't have the technology for individual laser guns. Also, the descriptions he gave of the type of wounds inflicted by the weapons match top-secret test data, too."

"You mean he may not be lying?"

"The CIA has been with him at the hospital for two days, and I saw him for several hours. He won't change his story."

"Well, if what he says is true . . ."

"Then he's talking about a buildup of extremely advanced weaponry in an isolated area dangerously close to the U.S. mainland," Smith said grimly.

"A secret army?" Remo asked.

Smith held out his hands. "An army, a military base, an espionage station . . . It could be anything."

"What does the Guatemalan government say?"

"They categorically deny the presence of any

foreign military power on their territory," Smith said. "Under the circumstances, the President of the United States can't risk sending in armed troops to investigate. That's where you come in."

"To check things out."

"To confirm or deny Diehl's allegations. If there are laser weapons in use, we want one of them. And of course you'll do what you can to stop any possible encroachment of enemy troops toward the United States."

Remo said, "Does it have to be a jungle?"

"You were looking forward to going a few minutes ago," Smith said, standing up. "You'll leave tomorrow morning on a commercial flight to Guatemala City. After that, you'll have to make your own way. A large part of your journey will be on foot, I'm afraid."

"Excellent," Chiun said. "He can use the exercise."

CHAPTER THREE

There was something about the jacaranda tree that looked familiar. Possibly because the Peten jungle was full of jacaranda trees. Possibly because the greenery in the region of Guatemala where Remo and Chiun were walking had been growing, steadily and uninterrupted, for the past 20 million years and offered barely enough light at four o'clock in the afternoon to see two feet in front of them. Possibly because Remo and Chiun walked without leaving tracks.

If they had been ordinary men, the damp, overgrown earth beneath their feet would have been crumpled and squashed, and their every move would have left marks. But the teachings of Sinanju had ingrained in both the old Oriental and the young American an instinct for balance that permitted them to move without a trace.

So it took Remo several hours to realize that

they had been traveling in a continuous circle around the familiar looking jacaranda.

"Balls," said Remo, who was unwise in the ways of philosophical thought.

"At last," said Chiun, who was not.

Remo looked, stony faced, to the old man. "You knew we were walking in a circle?"

"Please," Chiun said wearily. "How often must one fall from the hump of a horse to realize he is riding a camel?"

"Huh?"

"The scent of the river. It grows weaker and stronger as one walks toward and away from it. The shadows on the leaves move with direction as well as time. There were a hundred signs pointing the way to our destination. A thousand clues . . ."

"And one map," Remo added, "which you gave to the stewardess on the plane."

"It was not the map I gave the lovely lady who recognized the Master of Sinanju and was concerned for his privacy."

The Pan Am stew's concern for Chiun's privacy centered around a Barbra Streisand movie being shown in the cabin, for which several other passengers refused to sit in reverent silence. One of those passengers decided to maintain an appropriate attitude after discovering that his head had been stuffed in one of the plane's toilets. Another found the pleasures of silence when he was packed neatly into the seat cushion of the passenger immediately in front of him.

The captain, who did not at first understand

Chiun's desire to watch the movie in peace, finally agreed that the old man had a point. He arrived at this revelation while hanging by his fingertips from a window of the L-1011, flapping like a banner from the flying craft. Yes, indeed, the gentleman certainly did have a point there, the stewardess readily agreed as she evacuated the other passengers to seats in other cabins. Then she brought Chiun foot warmers and pillows and a box of chocolates donated by the passengers in the first-class cabin, who also understood that the Master of Sinanju wished to hear Barbra Streisand's golden tones without the babble of unappreciative louts.

"It was too the map. You wrote something on the back of it and handed it to her. I saw you."

"It was paper. On it I wrote one of the finest verses of Wang, the poet and greatest Master of Sinanju. It was something she would treasure in the dreariness of her life."

"The map on the other side of it was something I would have treasured, too."

"You are impossible," Chiun said. "I raise you from a nothing—less than nothing, a white man—but do I get even a single shred of respect for my efforts? Did I receive even a thank you when you demanded that I, an old man in the twilight of my life, leap from a moving airplane?"

"We had to jump out of the plane because every bureaucrat in Guatemala was at the airport waiting to deport us. Smitty would've loved that. And it wasn't like it was flying. It was taxiing."

Chiun sniffed. "Not even a thank you."

"Thank you, Chiun," Remo said elaborately. "Thank you for taking the map out of my pocket after I'd already jumped out of the plane and it was too late to take it back."

"It was nothing," Chiun said, smiling sweetly.

Remo exhaled noisily. "Well, there's no point in arguing about the map. It's gone."

"A map is unnecessary."

"But we don't know where we're going," Remo explained. "I only remember that it was somewhere west of Progresso, in the jungle. Here we are. Information terminated."

"We could ask."

"Oh, sure. We've been tramping around this overgrown greenhouse all day. We haven't seen so much as a chipmunk."

"You haven't," Chiun said. "But that is to be expected. You also did not see the tree we passed three times."

Remo tossed down the empty canvas bag he was carrying. "Okay, I give up," he said. "Show me this mysterious traffic cop of the jungle. I'll ask directions."

Chiun nodded. Through the dense brush, Remo could make out a form moving with the subtle signs of human breathing. It was a man, old by the sound of him. He was wearing a loose brown garment of some kind and was bent over at the waist, as if examining something on the ground. In his hands were bunches of white flowers.

"You were right," Remo said, amazed.

"Again," Chiun said off-handedly.

"Hey there, excuse me," Remo shouted. He made it a habit of announcing himself wherever he wanted to be seen approaching. Otherwise, he'd discovered, he seemed to materialize out of nowhere, usually scaring out of their socks whoever it was he wanted to talk to. It didn't make for good first impressions.

"Holy shit," the old man said, his hand on his heart. "You scared the socks off me. You American?"

Remo nodded. "You?"

The old man held up two fingers, making the peace sign. "Sebastian Birdsong. First Church of Krishna the Undraftable, Los Angeles, California. Peace, man."

Birdsong looked as if he were forty going on seventy. His gray shoulder-length hair was matted with dreadlocks, the result of years of wear without benefit of comb or shampoo. One hoop earring glinted from his right ear. Over his stooped shoulders was draped a cotton caftan, which had once been orange, sporting a paisley design, but had degenerated through unwashed ages to a stiff, uniformly gray-brown color, its sleeves frayed to the elbow. On his feet were crumbling leather strips that had once been a pair of sandals.

"Birdsong?" Remo asked.

The man smiled, exposing two rows of rotten teeth resembling dried corn. "It used to be Humberbee, but I changed it," he said. "In the First Church of Krishna the Undraftable, they let you pick your own names. It's like freedom, man. Groovy. Really boss."

"Groovy?" It had been years since Remo had heard anything described as groovy.

"Yeah. Far out. Like wicked, man. A rush. A righteous groove. In the congregation, we got Daffodils, Butterflies, Seagulls—lots of Seagulls. Last time I looked, we had forty-two girls—I mean, women—named Seagull. The Church doesn't allow us to say 'girls.' It's a repressive buzzword of the male chauvinist elitist power-mongers. Last time I was at church, they baptized twelve six-pound women. All named Seagull. 'Dove's' big, too," he pondered. Like for the Dove of Peace, dig it? Like it's an anti-war statement, like."

"Anti which war?"

Birdsong looked at him in astonishment. "*The* war, you apolitical stooge of the military industrialist bourgeoisie. The *Vietnam* war. The toy of the capitalist powermongers. The genocidal elitist—"

"That war's over," Remo said.

Birdsong's eyes widened. "It's over? Over?" He clasped Remo's hand, smearing his palm with the sticky juice from the white flowers he carried. "Well, don't just stand there, man. Like rejoice! It's over!"

"It's been over for ten years," Remo said.

Birdsong didn't seem to hear him. "Over! It's over! I can go home now. Outasight." He danced in a wild fury, undulating his hips and pretending to play an imaginary electric guitar.

"How long have you been here, anyway?" Remo asked.

Birdsong counted backward on his fingers. "Let me see. This is August, so July, June . . . fifteen years."

"Fifteen years? You mean you've been here since the sixties?"

"Right on, man." He winked. "Fuckin' A I've been here. Alive and breathing. Not diced and wok-fried, you dig? Not shot, bayonetted, grenaded, mined, gassed, stabbed, or dead of Charlie's creepy crawlies. I'm free."

Remo, who was a veteran, suppressed an urge to crush the man's skull into oatmeal. "The church sent you here?" he asked.

"Missionary work," Birdsong said gleefully. "It was a great scam. You pay your bread to the main man, and the First Church of Krishna the Undraftable makes you a card-carrying missionary. Get to see the world and save your ass at the same time." His smile turned to an expression of bewilderment. "'Course, I haven't heard from the church since 1969. They never did tell me how I was going to get out of here. Guess they didn't think of that part."

Remo noticed the subtle darkening of the trees. Night was falling, and he was wasting time talking to this aging hippie draft dodger. "Listen—do you know your way around here? My friend and I are lost."

"Friend? What friend?" Birdsong gave a little squeal as Chiun seemed to materialize out of nowhere. "Wow, you guys sure come up quick," he said. "Say, what direction did you come from?"

Chiun pointed behind him.

Birdsong held up the bunch of white flowers. "See any of these before you split?"

"A few," Chiun said. "Not many."

"Didn't think so," the man said with dismay. "They're rare nowadays. Pain in the ass to pick. I'm taking care of a kid, got a bad leg. Claims these make him feel better."

"About the directions," Remo said.

"I mean, I'm a missionary, right?" Birdsong went on, apparently unused to conversing with anyone other than himself. "One crippled kid. Some mission."

"Do you have a dwelling for your services?" Chiun asked politely.

"Hell, no," Birdsong said. "Seventeen thatched huts. That's what I had, and every single one of them burned down. The jerks around here don't go for missionaries. Hocus pocus, that's what they want. Geez, give me a hundred tabs of acid, and I'll have more followers than Ringo Starr. One gimp kid." He threw up his arms. "Well, that's over with now. I'm going to find my way out of this dump, and then it's hello Sunset Boulevard."

"About the directions," Remo repeated.

"Yeah? Where you cats going?"

Chiun's jaw tightened. "We cats are searching for what is known as the Temple of Magic. But my apprentice here was so foolish as to keep the map on the reverse side of valuable poetry, and so we are now without directions."

Remo sighed.

Birdsong looked up, his eyes round. "The Temple of Magic?" he asked softly. His open mouth formed into a tense smile. "Hey, man. You don't want to go there."

"Why not?" Remo asked.

"Well, like I don't want to put you on a scare trip, you know? But they got these people here, they don't like white folks."

"A very enlightened population," Chiun said, beaming. "I knew there was something about this place I liked."

"They don't like other folks much, either. Not even the other Indians."

"They're natives?"

"Nobody knows where they come from. They paint little black dots on their foreheads, and man, when you see those dots, you better split fast."

"And if I do not divide?" Chiun asked.

"Then you'll be looking death right in the eye," Birdsong said sagely. "Even the local Indians, and they've been living in the jungle here for thousands of years now, don't know who these guys are. They call them the Lost Tribes. There's some kind of legend that they were driven off their land by a kingdom run by white gods, and they've been wandering around the jungle ever since, punishing everybody and his brother for it."

"When did this happen?"

"Who knows?" Birdsong said. "The locals say the Lost Tribes got lost at the beginning of time. All I know is, those suckers are mean. Every last one of my seventeen missions burned to the ground."

"The Lost Tribes did that?"

Birdsong expelled a little puff of air. "I was lucky. At least they didn't kill me. Those freaking wild men slink around the jungle like jaguars. Whenever they come across a settlement, it's open season. Out come their peashooters and spears, zap, zap, adios homestead, you dig? Then it's off into the jungle again till the next time they feel like shrinking some heads."

"What's that got to do with the Temple of Magic?" Remo asked.

"That's one of their crash pads or something. God knows why. I've never seen it, but the natives say the place is a wreck. Hasn't been used in a zillion years. But go there, and the Lost Tribes'll be swarming over you like flies at a chocolate orgy. Like killing's their thing, man. Matter of fact, a bunch of white folks just got creamed over there."

"Yeah, we've heard."

"They were some kind of archaeologists or something. When I found out they were headed for the Temple of Magic, I took off after them, to warn them, like. But they got too close to the place, and I sure as hell didn't want to follow anybody into a massacre. Like that's why I never volunteered for Vietnam, man. Screw that murder shit, I said. 'Specially when it's me that's going to get murdered. I came back to the mission. It was the sixteenth mission, I think. Maybe the fifteenth. But I was dead right in coming back. Couple of days later, I got word that the Lost Tribes sent every last one of them on the ultimate cosmic trip. It was Croak City for all of them. You dig what I'm saying, man? Like the Temple of Magic is an A-one bummer."

"We can look after ourselves," Remo said.

"Suit yourselves," Birdsong said. "It's that way." He pointed in a direction vaguely northeast of the river. "Don't bother looking for it now, though."

"Why not?"

"Too dark. It's a half-day's walk, maybe more. And the Lost Tribes come out at night." He slid a finger across his throat, accompanied by appropriate facial gestures. "I've got to get out of here myself. Never can tell when those bastards'll get the urge to waste somebody."

Gingerly he gathered up a few more of the delicate white flowers. "You can come back to the mission with me if you want. Nothing there but burned ground and a few reeds, but it's home for me and the kid. Say, you haven't seen him anyplace, have you? Little skinny kid, about twelve years old, walks with a limp?"

"Sorry," Remo said. "We've got to get moving. Thanks for the directions."

"Big mistake," Birdsong said with a shrug. "Well, see you in the obituary pages." He laughed.

"Draft dodger," Remo muttered under his

breath as they veered away from Birdsong into the darkness of the jungle.

"He smelled like a hippo. What is a draft dodger?" Chiun asked, eyeing the bent figure of the missionary over his shoulder.

"Someone who sneaks out of serving his country when it needs him."

Chiun's eyebrows arched. "For purposes of killing?"

"For purposes of being a soldier."

"In the army?"

"Right. The army," Remo said distractedly, clearing a path for them in the indigo-colored jungle. Overhead the night birds screeched.

They trod gently through the dense, blackening brush, dotted sparsely with white flowers. "Had this Birdsnest not dodged the drafty army, would he have become like the soldiers we have seen at military bases?"

"Sort of. The ones we've seen lately have been volunteers. The draft was a duty. That hoople picking the flowers wouldn't know duty from fly droppings," Remo said. "First Church of Krishna the Undraftable. Sheesh."

"He was right," Chiun said solemnly.

"Oh, come on. He was a jerk."

Chiun thought. "That, too. But he was right. No government should resort to hiring amateur assassins when professionals are available. How many casualties did your side inflict during this contest?"

"It wasn't a contest. It was a war. A long, bloody war."

"How many casualties?" Chiun insisted.

"Oh, I don't know," Remo said irritably. "A lot. Hundreds of thousands."

Chiun gasped. "Hundreds of thousands! Imagine how much revenue that would have brought to the glorious House of Sinanju. And the job would have been done right. No booms. Three or four days, tops. Of course, one would have to charge extra for overtime. . . ."

"The war's over," Remo said.

"And all the potential profits gone," Chiun lamented. "One commission like that, and catastrophe in my village may have been averted. Alas, the people of Sinanju will have to live in fear forever, hoping that their Master can earn enough tribute to keep starvation from their doors. For without the gold I send them, the people of Sinanju would go hungry, and be forced—"

"I know, I know. Forced to send their babies back to the sea."

Chiun stopped, placing his hands on his hips. His face was set to the mode Remo recognized as "Righteous Indignation." "There are many things a soft white man would find impossible to believe, many hardships and sufferings which are commonplace in the world."

"I believe you, Little Father," Remo said, tempering his weariness and frustration with as much gentleness as he could muster. "It's just that I've heard it before. How the village was so poor that people had to drown their infants to ward off starvation. How the first Master of

Sinanju saved the village by renting out his services as an assassin to foreign governments. How Sinanju possessed nothing but the secrets of the sun source of the martial arts, known only to the Master. How each succeeding Master has carried on the tradition by offing the enemies of whatever emperor was paying him at the time."

"It is all true," Chiun said stubbornly.

"I know it's true. But it happened thousands of years ago. Sinanju at this moment is about as poverty stricken as Houston."

"Still, one must be on one's guard," Chiun grumbled.

"I'll keep an eye out."

"It is too late. The opportunity has already been missed. Hundreds of thousands."

"There'll be another war someday," Remo said consolingly.

Chiun's face brightened. "Really? Do you really think so?"

"There's always hope, Little Father," Remo said. "Little Father?" He backtracked to where Chiun was sitting, inexplicably, on the ground. "You feel all right?"

"I'm fine," Chiun said, yawning. "But the day has been long, and I am an old man. I grow weary."

"I've never seen you grow weary before." Remo changed his position to match the old Oriental's full lotus. Suddenly he realized that he, too, felt tired. No, not tired. Despite the heat and the dampness and the long day's walk, his muscles were still taut and performing well. If they hadn't been, the remedy would have been food, not rest. Both their bodies were long used to functioning on a fraction of the rest ordinary people needed.

No, it was something in his eyes, in his brain. Something cloudy and pleasant and reminiscent of childhood. "I think I'm sleepy," Remo said.

"HNNNNNNNK," Chiun responded.

Remo looked around. The ground was spotted heavily with the strange white flowers Birdsong had been gathering. He'd never seen any like them before, dainty, fragrant. His brain in a haze, he reached over and picked one. Its fluted petals were soft and fat, juicy with fragrance. He held it up to his nose, crushing it inadvertently with fingers grown suddenly clumsy as he brought the blossom closer.

The odor, thick and inviting, jolted him like the injection of a narcotic. The forest swirled above him, dark and sweet and protective. It would be hard for even the Lost Tribesmen to find him here, he thought with his last strands of consciousness. Well, just a little nap, maybe. Too dark to make good time walking, anyway. Not to mention the pain in the ass it would be to have to fight of a bunch of thrill-crazed natives at the Temple of Magic now, when all he wanted was a minute or two of shut-eye.

"Hey, Chiun," he slurred, flinging over an uncontrollable hand at the small sleeping figure. "Chiun, we can't sleep here too long. The Lost Tribes. Got to keep an eye out. Missed opportunities. Might be a war or something; Sinanju could strike it rich." His words came slower and softer. "Got to wake up, Chiun. We don't need the ultimate cosmic journey. Chiun . . ."

"HNNNNNNNK."

"Okay," Remo agreed.

He awoke to a scream.

It was dawn. Chiun was already up, his limbs relaxed into fighting position. Instantly the foggy stupor of Remo's senses cleared, his reflexes overtaking the soporific effect of the white flowers now that they were needed for action.

Remo thrust his chin toward the river, where he thought the sound had originated. The gesture was a question. Chiun answered it with a silent nod.

The trail was easy to find. The dense underbrush of the jungle lay flattened where three pairs of feet had crushed it, less than a hundred yards from where he and Chiun had lain asleep during the night. Two sets were normal, each foot touching the ground with approximately the same weight as the other. The third set was lighted and uneven, as if one foot had dragged while the other stepped. A wounded man, perhaps. A small man.

He shivered. He had not heard a sound during the night, had never wakened once. His body was alert to danger, and there was no chance that his reflexes wouldn't have served him in a life-threatening situation. There were just some things you had to trust; Remo's was his body. But the fact that he'd been able to sleep through the noisy passage of three people easily within normal human earshot made him uneasy. He would take back some of the flowers to Smith for analysis. Whatever was in those fat, fragrant petals was strong stuff. If it could knock him and Chiun out, it could drug an army.

The forest thinned as they neared the river. Heat from the dappled sunlight through the leaves overhead burned into his shoulders. By dawn, it was already eighty degrees.

He paused. Sound. Not three men. No footfalls. The only movement besides the motion of the river and the rustling of birds and small creatures was coming from straight ahead, in the clearing by the banks of the river.

One man, he was sure of it. Alone.

He stepped past Chiun and parted the leaves of a eucalyptus. He waited there for a moment, seeing the elements of the picture in front of him, but not understanding. And then he understood, and wished he didn't.

On the far bank of the river, beneath the overhanging branch of a tree, swung the body of Sebastian Birdsong. A handmade hemp rope was twisted around his neck. Birdsong's eyes were bulging with black swarms of flies. His bare feet just touched the surface of the river, parting it into two rippling V's. On the rocks and mud of the riverbank were scattered the white flowers Birdsong had picked.

Standing next to the body, propped on three flat stones piled to make a step, was a boy. He was young, no more than twelve years old, with the black, coarse hair and brown skin of the Guatemalan. He wore only a small cloth between his legs. On his left knee was a gray rag bandage. Birdsong's kid, Remo thought. His one convert.

The boy held a thick knife in his hands. With one hand he steadied the rope supporting Birdsong's body, while he sawed at it with the other. He stopped when Remo and Chiun walked out onto the riverbank. For a moment, his knife hand came in close to his chest, waiting for the two strangers to attack. But they waited, watching, not moving.

After a few moments, his eyes never leaving the silent figures of Remo and Chiun, the boy raised his hands to the rope again.

Chapter Four

They didn't venture near the boy. Instead, Remo dug a deep grave in the soft earth beside the river bank, opposite where the boy stood cutting down the old man's body. When the boy finished and Birdsong's remains lay in the shallows of the water, he looked for a moment to the two strange men on the far side of the river. One was white, like Father Sebastian. He was younger than the white priest, taller, thinner, yet he carried a weight in him that the white Father had not possessed. Something deep within his eyes, a strength.

The old man had the strength, too, even though he looked to be very old, older than the boy had ever imagined a man could become. In the hills where he had lived with his parents, no one grew to be old. The fever took them, or the spirits of the evil ones. Or the Lost Tribes. They had taken many.

Before his father died, he had spoken to the

boy in the Old Tongue now used only by the hill people who lived apart from the villagers. His family spoke Mayan, too, but for special occasions, for weighty matters, the Old Tongue was used. It was the language of the ancients, of the great ones, the speech of those who had seen the coming of the white god Kukulcan in his flaming chariot. The Old Tongue had been spoken since the beginning of time, and it carried magic.

The people who lived in villages no longer understood magic. They held their ceremonies to Chac, the rain god, and consulted the village *h'men*, the priest with the power, when there was sickness in their families, but there was no more magic. The ancient temples had been left to fall into ruin, overrun by white men with their gadgets and papers, and they had forgotten the language of magic, the Old Tongue with which their ancestors had talked with gods.

But the hill people had not forgotten. And when the boy's father had called him beside the reed mat where he lay dying, his eyes glistening with the killing fever, he had used the ancient language to bless the boy.

"Be strong, for you alone will walk with the gods," he had said.

The boy had wondered then if that meant that he would die next. He did not fear death. He had watched two sisters and an infant brother die, and it had not seemed a terrible thing. There were many deaths in the village, too, and when he had taken the vegetables his father grew and the woven mats his mother made to the village to exchange for a chicken or a ceramic bowl, he had seen the death ceremonies where women wept and the *h'men* chanted, and could not understand why something so commonplace as death should be treated with such grief.

His father had died after he spoke with his son, and then the boy and his mother carried the body from the house to bury it while the younger children looked on. And while he buried his father, the boy guessed that he would die soon, too.

He was not strong. Though he was the oldest child, he was only barely taller than his brother who was three years younger. And then there was his leg. It was malformed at birth, and his father had broken the bone at the knee to straighten the leg. Perhaps the remedy had worked. He could walk, at least, although the pain in his knee was often so great that he lost consciousness. His mother had kept the knee wrapped with poultices made of the white flowers that grew in the terrible parts of the jungle, and that helped. But the pain was always there.

No, death would not be so bad.

But it was not he who died. After the rainy season passed, while he tried to cultivate the land washed down to clay by the heavy rains, the Lost Tribes had come with their spears and knives and their own magic, the spears of light that their people, according to legend, had stolen from the gods themselves at the beginning of time.

He had spotted them, running out of the jungle brush like savage cats, lithe, menacing. He moved as fast as he could to warn his mother and his brothers and sisters.

What would that have done, he wondered later. Where could they have gone? The Lost Tribes were swift, and they wished only to kill. There was no place to hide from them. But he tried to reach his kin.

If he had reached them, they would have died together. But his bad leg moved slowly, and the warriors of the Lost Tribes were on him before he could even shout to the house. One of them slashed the boy's arm with a knife. The boy rolled down the rocky hill, sliding, skidding. He landed on a heavy rock, square on his knee. The pain had surged through him like a flood, sending bile shooting up into his mouth and the ringing, throbbing red pain into his head. And then the blackness had come.

When he awakened, they were all dead. His mother, three sisters, four small boys. The village had been attacked, too, the first of the attacks on the village.

Father Sebastian had found him several days later, grubbing at roots and eating leaves. His arm had grown swollen and painful, and his knee hurt so much that the boy had chipped one of his teeth as he tightened his mouth to bear the pain.

Father Sebastian was not a strong man, but he had kindness. He had saved his life. He had fed him and kept him with him.

And now he was dead, too, the boy thought, numbly. He could not live in the jungle alone, not with a leg that was like a beast gnawing at him. Certainly none of the villagers would take him in. A lame boy, one more mouth to feed. All that was left for him was a swift death by the Lost Tribes, if he was lucky. If he was not, then it would be a slow death, starvation, fever, mauling by baboons. Or death by the two stange men on the opposite side of the riverbank, the young white man and the old creature who was not like any man he had ever seen. He looked like a prophet.

Or a god.

They did not beckon to him, did not speak. The hole the white man had dug must be a grave. It was the right size and shape. What else could it be?

But why would they help bury Father Sebastian?

As the boy watched the still, silent men, still with a quiet that was almost not human, so precisely unmoving that the very air seemed to swirl and thunder around them, one word came to him, a name from the sacred sounds of the Old Tongue: *Kukulcan.*

Kukulcan, the white god. Kukulcan, magic one, he of the flaming chariot come to lead his ancestors to greatness. As old as the wind by now. As old as the strange old man across the river.

"Kukulcan," he said softly, then dragged the

body of Father Sebastian through the shallows toward the grave.

"What'd he say?" Remo asked.

Chiun wasn't listening. His eyes were on the boy as he dragged his heavy burden toward them.

It was Chiun who had insisted that they let the boy come to them. To approach him would have only frightened him away, and there was danger in the jungle for a child alone, even an Indian child who knew his way.

And there was something else, something special about this boy. It showed around his eyes and mouth. Serenity, for one so young. Strength, perhaps. Possibility. Not possibility in Remo's way; the boy was lame. He could never learn the ways of Sinanju. But his eyes had met Chiun's, and in them the old man had seen something rare and ancient.

"Let me help him," Remo said.

"There is no need."

The boy dragged the body to the gravesite, his head down. He raised it only once, to look at Chiun. The old Oriental nodded, then took Birdsong's body from the boy and lifted it over the open grave.

Birdsong was nearly twice Chiun's size, yet the old Oriental handled him as if he were made of cotton, holding him aloft, closing his eyes and mouth and arranging his clothing with hands so swift, they seemed to move in a blur. When he laid the body in the grave, it appeared to float into the waiting earth. Remo covered it.

The boy said nothing.

"Okay, kid, it's been a rough day for you," Remo said, slapping the last particles of dirt from his hands. "Let's get you home."

"Imbecile," Chiun said. "He lived with the dead person. The person's mission burned down. He said so himself."

"The village, then. We've got to get him to the village. Wherever that is." He turned back to the boy. "Village," he enunciated carefully. "Town. People. Coca Cola." He pointed in several different directions, querying with his eyes. "Village that way? There?"

The boy was silent.

"Oh, hell," Remo said. "We'll have to take him back to Progresso. We'll miss at least three days getting to the temple. Well, come on, then." He reached absently for the boy's arm.

The boy skittered away. Standing a few feet away, he stared at Remo. There was no way to tell what the child was thinking. His dark eyes conveyed nothing. Not fear, not hope, not sadness. Nothing. It was as if he were waiting for something. But what?

"That's one funny kid," Remo said. "What does he want?"

"He will let us know," Chiun said.

"Well, I'm not in the mood for playing games." Remo walked toward the boy. "Now listen. We've got to find a way to get you to somebody who'll take care of you, understand? You can't stay here by yourself. And you sure can't come with us. The Temple of Magic is off limits to you."

The boy ran away, limping, his leg dragging behind him as he disappeared into the soggy marsh of the riverbank.

Chiun placed a restraining hand on Remo's arm. "Let him go," he said.

"Are you crazy? We can't leave a crippled kid alone out here. You saw what whoever-it-was did to Birdsong."

Chiun turned away and began to walk delicately through the brush.

"Didn't you hear me, Little Father? We can't leave him alone."

"He is not alone," Chiun said.

Remo ran to catch up with him. "You're talking in riddles again. He looked alone to me. Who's with him?"

"We are." He nodded toward the left. Two dark eyes peered out of the foliage. A small hand beckoned them forward. When they arrived at the spot where the boy had stood, he was gone, staring at them from a place beyond.

"He is leading us to the temple."

"We can find our own way," Remo said. "This is no place for a kid."

Chiun sighed. "You forget, my son. He has lived here all his life."

"We can't be responsible for him."

"And so, then, to whom are we responsible?" Chiun's withered old face was suddenly, passionately full of emotion. "I carry the responsibility of a whole village upon my shoulders each day.

For whom do you toil, my son? For yourself, who has no family, no home? For me, who already possesses the skills of a thousand men? For your Emperor Smith, perhaps, who loves a country, but cannot see the faces of the people who make up that country?"

A heavy feeling settled into Remo's chest. He did not like to be reminded that he was an outcast. An orphan, raised by nuns. A soldier, returning from a hideous war to no one. A policeman, framed and scapegoated by his peers. And now an assassin with no official identity, no friends, no family. He had been born, it seemed, to dance on the fringes of humanity, never touching the real people of the real world.

"Don't get philosophical on me," he said thickly.

The boy beckoned. They followed.

"He needs a doctor or something," Remo said. "He can hardly walk."

"And yet he struggles to keep ahead of us," Chiun said.

It was true. Through the orchestra of sound that pervaded the jungle at full daylight, Remo could make out the boy's raspy breathing. He was gasping as his footfalls fell harder and more unevenly with each step.

"True strength is not in the muscles of the body," Chiun said. "It is something in the mind, a power that makes the muscles work beyond endurance. That is the difference between man and beast. It is what separates the teachings of

Sinanju from the trickery of the lesser martial arts. The boy has strength. The Master respects that."

"Even if he dies?" Remo said with more than a touch of sarcasm.

"Death comes to us all at the appointed time," Chiun said simply. "The boy knows that. Why don't you?"

"For Pete's sake, he's a child. A baby."

"And he is showing us the way," Chiun said, following the trembling, beckoning hands of the boy.

They walked for several hours, the boy darting ahead, silent, waiting. The jungle changed color from green to indigo again, the sunlight blocked out by the thickening foliage.

"One thing I'd like to know," Remo said. "Why are you making such a big deal about this kid? You act like you know him."

"Perhaps I do," Chiun said cryptically. "There is something in his eyes. Maybe what I see there is all the children of Sinanju who were sent back to the sea."

Remo took a deep breath. "If there's one thing I can't stand, it's Oriental sentimentality," he said.

There was a crackle in the forest, nearby. Feet, many feet moving swiftly, intakes and outrushes of breath. The boy's ragged gasp. Chiun leaping ahead like a bird, grasping the boy in one swift motion, hurling the child behind him to safety. Remo's reflexes, like lightning, shooting through his body, melting it to liquid, moving it smoothly, automatically.

Seconds expanding into hours. Time, time enough for everything as Remo's body readied, his senses taking in everything, his mind sorting, storing, reacting. The men—six of them—their naked bodies brown and tough as leather, their faces stained with color to make them look ferocious. At the center of each brown forehead was a black ash dot, the tribal marking.

The Lost Tribes. They fought, not like modern men with soft hands and clumsy legs, but like jungle fighters. Smooth, interchangeable cogs, surrounding the two of them, a circle of black dots, like third eyes peering from the dense greenery. Their weapons were primitive but wielded with precision. The first spear was aimed at Chiun. He caught it in midair and turned it, in the same movement, on the attackers. One fell, screaming. The others did not even seem to notice. The knives came. Slingshots filled with sharp stones.

They kept away. No hand-to-hand. No way to use Sinanju until they were close enough. But they would be close enough. A frontal rolling attack, two of them at once, and . . .

Remo stopped cold. Two men stepped out in a blaze of the whitest light Remo had ever seen. Behind Chiun, giant trees crashed to earth like broken toothpicks. Yards of moss and dense, low plants turned into smoldering black goo.

In the warriors' hands were weapons. They vaguely resembled the M-16s used during the Vietnam war, but they were sleeker, cleaner looking. The metal they were made of was green and sparkling with newness. The men handled them as if they were made of balsa wood, tossing them onto their shoulders with delicate deftness. When they fired, there was no explosion, no crack as bullets shot out from the barrel. Except for a whining *ping* like the sounds on a television video game, the weapons worked in silence, sending out beams of blinding light.

"Lasers," Remo whispered, marveling at the destruction wrought by the two weapons.

"Move," Chiun commanded. "Match me."

Automatically Remo obeyed, his body moving opposite Chiun's, circling, crouching, leaving the ground in what would have been a flying tackle if there had been less flying.

They moved so fast that the men with the weapons hadn't even turned their heads to follow them when the assault came, crumpling the two warriors into one another, kicking out at the others who rushed to their flanks, circling, moving, always moving, a cracked spine, a crushed skull, two fingers in the windpipe, a kick that turned one warrior's intestines to jelly.

A weapon was pointed directly at Remo. One stroke, and it lay on the ground in shards. Metal was easy enough to break, but this metal had shattered as if it had been made of glass. Remo finished the man off with a snap of the neck, and then everything was still.

"These things fell apart like Tinker Toys," Remo said, picking up the shattered fragments of the weapon. Only one remained whole. Remo fired experimentally into the air. With a *ping*, a shaft of light blazed in a visible line from the barrel to the sky. Everything in its path—leaves, branches, even a low cloud—disintegrated. The cloud rumbled once, distant thunder, and then dissipated into thin air. "Well, it works," Remo said.

He placed it in the empty bag he carried, proof for Smith. "Whoever made this thing is light years ahead of us, only . . ." He squeezed the butt of the rifle between his thumb and his forefinger. It crumbled beneath his touch as if it were made of paper. What kind of weapon was this, sending deadly power from a casing as fragile as butterfly wings?

The boy stepped cautiously out of the brush. His face looked pale beneath the sun-browned skin, his dark eyes wide.

"Do not be afraid, my child," Chiun said gently, extending his arms. The boy took two steps nearer, his left leg dragging uselessly behind the right. Then his eyes rolled back into his head and he fainted.

"Fools," Chiun said angrily. "We have both been fools." He bent over the boy and propped him up in his arms. "He no doubt has not eaten for two days or more. He needs food. Go find us fish, Remo."

"Fish? We left the river six hours ago."

"It has wound around this way," Chiun said stubbornly. "I can smell it."

Chiun carefully unwrapped the bandage around the boy's knee. Inside, next to the skin, was a poultice made of hundreds of the white flowers he and Remo had seen the night before. They were crushed and fragrant, their effect making Chiun dizzy. He slowed his breathing, watching the boy take in the quieting fumes as he slept. His leg was mangled, hurt beyond repair. The boy would never walk normally.

His parents must have been compassionate indeed, Chiun thought. Few outside of the "civilized" countries of the world, where everyone was forced to live long lives while encouraged to poison themselves with bad food and alcohol and tobacco and medical drugs and worries, would have allowed this child to live. Small, maimed, silent.

Did he speak any language? Did he understand words at all? He must. He said something at the river, one word. Had it just been nonsense, the babbling of an idiot?

The sight of the boy tore at the old man's heart. This lame child, mute and doomed, unreachable, *was* the lost babies of Sinanju, all of the bright new lives that were never to be. By right, this boy should not have lived, either. But he had somehow escaped the Great Void to be with Chiun and Remo now.

The question was why. Chiun did not know the boy's destiny, but he knew, understood without words, that it was somehow tied in with his own.

He spotted a few of the flowers near where the boy lay. Keeping his breathing slow, he gathered them up and crushed them into a fine paste, which he smeared on a piece of silk torn from his kimono.

The boy had awakened when he got back. In the distance, he could see Remo returning, three fat fish in his hands. Chiun wrapped the bright blue bandage around the boy's knee and knotted it expertly. The boy followed him with his eyes.

"Why have we been brought together, my strange little one?" Chiun said softly. "Is it you who needs, or is it I?"

"It is my father's prophecy," the boy said.

Chiun sat up slowly, appraising the young face with its ancient eyes. "And who is your father?" he asked, exhibiting no surprise that the boy could talk.

"One who knew the Old Tongue," the boy said proudly. "He is dead, but I know the Old Tongue, too."

There was something hopeful in the boy's dark eyes. "And what is the Old Tongue?" Chiun asked.

"The language of the gods. Not this white language that the white priest taught me, but the true language. The language of power."

"Did your father have the power?"

"Yes. When he died."

"What did he say?"

"That I alone of my family would walk with the gods."

"I do not understand," Chiun said.

"Nor do I. Yet."

"Ah." Chiun did not press him. The child spoke like a man, firm, calm, sparing.

"That was why I had to come with you," the boy said with quiet urgency.

"Was the pain very great?"

"Yes." It was plain, true, simple.

"Is it bearable now?"

"It is always bearable. But it is better now. Thank you, Master."

"My name is Chiun."

"My name is Po."

"For crying out loud, you speak English," Remo said, throwing down the fish. "Why wouldn't you talk when I asked you where the village was?"

"I do not belong in the village," Po said. "I belong with you. For now. Until I have completed my journey."

Remo put his hands on his hips. "Will you listen to that?" he said. "What journey?"

"Make the fire," Chiun said. "We have things to discuss."

They roasted the fish over the open fire. While they ate, Po told them about his family, his meeting with Sebastian Birdsong, the invasions of the Lost Tribes.

The boy grew drowsy after eating, and the three of them sat quietly with their thoughts. It was then that they heard the sound, far and muffled, like the mewling of a cat. Remo sprang to his feet.

"No danger," Chiun said, frowning, trying to locate the source of the sound. It seemed to be buried. No footfalls, no breathing.

The boy shook himself awake. "I heard nothing," he said.

"You cannot hear what we hear. Where is the Temple of Magic?" Chiun asked.

The boy pointed toward the faint sound. "It is near."

Remo and Chiun sprang away like two animals. The boy pulled himself to his feet, amazed at the speed and grace of the two men.

No, not men, he said to himself. That is why they fight as they do. That is why they can run faster than the wind. These are beings like Kukulcan himself who walk with me.

He found a stick and used it to walk, easing some of the constant ache in his leg. Near the entrance to the temple was a crashed helicopter. The bodies inside had already decomposed nearly to bone. By the time he reached the moss-covered, debris-littered ruin, Remo and Chiun were already flinging away the huge stones like handfuls of sand as the sound inside grew louder.

There is nothing these two cannot do, Po thought in amazement. They can build a world if they wish.

He cocked his head. The sound was stronger from the rear of the pyramidal base, coming from behind a barricade of rock.

"It is here," he shouted.

The two men came around. "Listen," he said. "Dig here, and you will find it more quickly."

Both men immediately went to work on a

mammoth stone, their hands vibrating on the rock, their bodies angling for leverage.

They did not doubt me because of my youth, Po thought. I spoke truth, and they understood.

And when they lifted the great stone, the noise burst out of the rock as if it had been buried there for a thousand years.

Weeping. A woman weeping.

Chapter Five

Mad. I'm going mad.

Dr. Elizabeth Drake bit her fingers to calm herself down, but the screaming wouldn't stop. Her screaming. Her fingers were raw and bleeding from trying to keep herself under control, her voice hoarse, her hands shaking, the food exhausted, and she was going to die. The fear lurched out of her like a living thing, the scream filling up the icebox-sized space where she had lived in darkness for—how long? Days? Weeks?

Ever since Diehl ran out on her. Men. They sniffed around you like dogs until you needed them, and then they sprouted wings. Dick Diehl, the archaeologist. The scholar. The scientist.

The rat.

How dare he assume she was dead? How dare he run away to save his own skin while she lay trapped beneath twenty tons of rock?

She panted softly to ease the pain in her chest from the racking sobs, the screams that shook her until she gagged. On her hands and knees, she felt her way over to the pile of now empty knapsacks stuffed into one corner of the small space.

She knew where everything was. This was her world now, the tiny, dark space where she lived, and she knew every centimeter of it even without the flashlight she carried in her waistband. Ahead, beneath the jagged stone, were the knapsacks. When Diehl threw her to safety during the attack, she had landed on the pile of canvas bags containing the dig's food supply. That was a stroke of luck, the only one in this whole luckless expedition. Otherwise she would have starved to death.

With trembling fingers she undid the clasp of her own knapsack and extracted the plastic vial that had kept her sane during her endless imprisonment. One Valium. The last one.

So long, sanity. She popped it into her mouth and swallowed the pill dry. Then she closed the clasp and replaced the knapsack where it had been.

A place for everything, and everything in its place. To the left of the knapsacks, in the low area where you had to squat, was the toilet, reeking, fly-covered. My fellow Vassar classmates, if you could see me now. And to the right . . .

She never moved to the right. Not since she had first explored the darkness with the flashlight and found the body lying beside her, with its glassy eyes and pallid skin. The corpse's face was all that showed, poking out from under an enormous cut stone that had crushed out the man's life. She recognized him as one of the natives brought along on the expedition. She hadn't approached the body again. She hadn't had to. Its stink was a constant reminder to her that she was not alone.

It should have been you, Dr. Diehl, you cowardly creep.

No one had gotten out except for Diehl. He had escaped. Logic told her he had. She had heard Diehl shouting her name when the earthquake first shook loose the temple and buried her in its rubble. And then she'd heard the shots, those strange little *pings* straight out of *Star Wars*, firing in the opposite direction. And then the thunder of the rest of the temple coming down, cutting off the wild native screams. Oh, God, the temple. The Temple of Magic, the greatest archaeological find since the Dead Sea Scrolls, oh no oh no oh no.

She dug her fingernails into her face. That was the last Valium, Drake, she told herself. Don't waste it.

Stifling a sob, she forced her mind to recount the events again. That was real; it happened; it would keep her sane. At least as long as the Valium held out.

The letter. First there was the letter from the expedition at the Temple of Magic, hinting at some great archaeological find. And the samples. Old. Older than anything she'd seen since the Oxkintok discoveries. The dig at Oxkintok had unearthed a Mayan lintel from 475 A.D., and the discovery had made history. It had also made Dick Diehl, who headed the expedition. a famous man.

Things had been terrific during that dig at Oxkintok. The thrill of discovery, the easy find, the cameraderie. She remembered the early morning coffee sessions when she and Diehl would go over the work for the day, the jokes, Diehl's easy smile. The evenings when, exhausted and so covered with dirt and ash that they looked like end men in a minstrel show, she and Diehl would amble over to the river and bathe in the cold, deep water while the sun set in a blaze over the Yucatan plains.

And the nights. The tension, lying in her tent wanting him, knowing he wanted her, too, trying to keep her mind on the dig while she grew wet with longing between her legs.

And then that wonderful moment when he'd unearthed the lintel, and they'd all gone crazy with excitement, kids at Christmas, dancing, shouting, everybody hugging everybody else. He'd kissed her then. It had just been the joy of the moment for both of them, embarrassing later, never discussed, but when he'd taken her in his arms and put his mouth on hers, it had been the most beautiful moment of her life.

He'd stayed, wrapped in her warmth, not wanting to let go. Until he'd said those magic words.

"Let's catalogue this stuff right away."

Mr. Romantic. Not "Darling, at last," not

"Come with me." Not even "Let's fuck." He wanted to catalogue the frigging lintel.

So they had. And it had been war since then. If Dick Diehl was going to be the supreme archaeologist, then, by God, Elizabeth Drake could out-professionalize him any day. They'd been competitors at UCLA after that, vying for the best digs, the most publications. She'd even topped him a few times. The fool. He hadn't even gotten mad. Her success seemed to please him, the jerk.

Everything was business with Diehl. Even when the two of them had reached the Temple of Magic and discovered the dead bodies of the entire crew from the first expedition, Diehl had gone immediately to the vases and bowls lining the walls, exclaiming that the temple was the most magnificent specimen of the Formative/Classic Mayan period since the burial vault discovered at Palenque.

She had stared at him then, wondering when he would take notice that twelve corpses were sprawled at his feet. But then everything happened so fast that it now seemed to her like a dream. A bad dream.

First came the tribesmen, primitive, frightening. They wore ash dots on their foreheads, and for a moment, all she could see was the ash dots, everywhere, it seemed, surrounding her like unseeing eyes.

And then the weapons. Wild things. Certainly not in keeping with the stone spears and crude metal knives they carried. Someone else was here, she reasoned. Some superpower plotting an invasion of North America? No, that was too James Bond to believe. Maybe an experimental American base, testing new weapons? It was a thought. She would certainly write to her congressman and the American Civil Liberties Union about it when she got back. No Defense Department was going to monkey around with exotic weapons in the middle of the most archaeologically significant region in the western hemisphere. A lot of people were going to hear from Elizabeth Drake when she got home.

Home.

Don't think about it, she told herself. One second at a time, that's how you've got to live now. No thinking ahead.

What came next? Oh, yes, the earthquake. The tribesmen were zapping the members of her expedition with these weird weapons, leaving holes the size of baseballs in their victims. Dick Diehl came for her then—who would have thought he cared—and threw her into the corner, against the knapsacks. The stuffed canvas bags broke her fall.

She thought the natives with the fancy guns were going to get Diehl for sure then, and she screamed. As if her scream were a prayer, it was answered by the earthquake.

She'd been too terrified to move. Rocks that had been standing for millennia suddenly toppled around her. Two giant square stones fell from directly overhead. It was a miracle that she hadn't been crushed on the spot.

A miracle, yes. They'd wedged against each other, forming a triangle above her head and scattering the other falling rocks to either side. As the earthquake continued to rumble, she could hear more rocks falling, burying her deeper. She could hear the screams of the tribesmen, crushed at the scene of their own destructiveness. Served them right. They all died except for Diehl. He got away.

The son of a bitch.

She could, even now, hear Dick Diehl calling her name. He'd had to run. She knew that, had known it then. He thought she was dead. Anyone would have died beneath the mountain of rock that fell onto her. It was just by pure chance—a whim of fate—that she had survived, unhurt.

Oh, God, let him have gotten away, the pompous, unromantic shitheel. Let Dick Diehl be safe.

The Valium was working. The screaming razor's edge was beginning to dull. Good, good. Maybe she would sleep. The less time spent conscious, the better. After all, she thought, it could be night. Maybe it was time to sleep.

A stone fell from above and skidded along her cheek. She gasped. Another stone. A fall of limestone powder.

The rocks. *They're giving away.*

More stones fell. She skittered to the far side of the area, opposite the knapsacks, and flattened herself against the wall. Another earthquake? Or just the normal shifting of things, an unseen hand moving the big rocks where they belonged, where they should have been all along. On top of her broken body.

Her face was wet. She realized that she was crying. No pleas to the Almighty now. This final irony didn't deserve them. Just tears, all the tears she'd been saving since she learned that serious women didn't cry. Go ahead and cry now, baby. It's time.

"Watch it. We don't want a landslide."

"What?" she said aloud. Someone was *out there.* The falling stones and dust must have opened an air passage in the far wall. And someone was there, there to help her, speaking English.

"I'm here!" she shouted. "In here!"

"She's in there," the voice said.

"Do you think I am deaf?" came another voice, a high singsong.

"Watch the rock."

"Watch your own rock. And straighten your elbow."

At least one of the men was an American. Could Dick Diehl have sent them? Was this a third expeditionary team? Oh, God, could Diehl be with them?

"Dick," she shrieked.

"Remo," came the voice.

"Chiun," came the other. "Greetings."

Greetings? What kind of way was that to talk to someone who'd been buried alive?

"Get me the fuck out of here," she yelled.

"Take it easy, girl. We'll get you."

He'd called her *girl.* She hated them already. Well, no point in being picky. She would deal with them later, report them to their superior. But at this point, they could be two redneck wifebeaters as far as she was concerned, as long as they got her out. Just keep coherent. Don't lose your head.

"There are two big stones, about two by two by four feet each, wedged in a triangle over my head," she said clearly.

"What did I tell you about your elbow?"

"Aw, lay off, Little Father. This isn't an exercise."

"All movement is exercise. Even the smallest motion should be performed correctly."

"All right. This way?"

"A little better. Not Korean, but better."

"Didn't you hear me?" Elizabeth Drake screamed.

"We heard you," Remo said.

"The yak drivers of the Himalayas could hear her," Chiun whispered. "The elbow."

A trickle of sand sifted down onto the archaeologist's head. "Watch what you're doing, you cretins!" she shouted.

"Look, you want us to come get you or not?"

"I want you to get me alive, idiot. Are you using pulleys?"

"An insult," the singsong voice said.

"We don't need them."

Crackpots. Her life was being entrusted to two lame-brains trying to dig her out with their bare hands. Graduate students, probably.

"Look, don't do me any favors by giving me a swift death. I'll hang on. Go into Progresso and get some pulleys or something. Maybe a crane, if there is one. I'll hang on."

"I told you, we can get you out," the American said. He sounded annoyed. Well, she had a hell of a lot more to be annoyed about than he did, the punk.

"And I told you to get some pulleys. Damn it, do this right, you fog-headed baboon."

"Come, Remo. We will leave this ungrateful wench."

"No," Dr. Drake gasped. "Don't leave. Please don't leave."

"Do you promise to be nice?" came the taunting American voice.

I'll be nice, she thought. Whoever that weirdo named Remo is, he'll see how nice I can be. With a nice kick into his nice nuts. "Just get me out of here," she said levelly.

Not that they could do it. No machinery, no levers. It was just her luck to be discovered by two macho male chauvinists who thought they could move a mountain of rock unassisted.

She settled back. Wonderful. This was just great. She couldn't be allowed to die quickly, by the guns the natives carried, oh, no. She couldn't die in the earthquake. The rocks that crushed the maggot-eaten thing on her right had to miss her. She wouldn't die of starvation. No. In the bizarre twists that fate had offered, she would survive all of those things so that she could be murdured by two half-wits trying to rescue her.

Well, fine. So be it. She was too tired to argue anymore. And the Valium was giving her a little buzz—not much, just enough to take the edge off a violent death. Screw it. She was going to lean back and get some sleep. It would be nice if the end came while she was unconscious. She'd always hoped to die in bed.

Then, just when things were swirling around her head nicely, the back fell out from behind her. She tumbled backward into fierce light. It took her eyes a few moments to adjust. The air was fragrant, moving. Sounds of wild creatures were everywhere, chirping, croaking, calling. She even thought she could hear the river. And the light, once she got used to it, was not blazing sunlight at all, but the soft, diffused light of the deep jungle. She smiled. Overhead were the fat leaves of eucalyptus trees and jungle rushes and . . . *people.* Two faces were staring down at her, one dumb-looking skinny young guy and an Oriental so old, he looked as if he were going to crumble to dust any second. And now a third face entered the strange picture above her, framed against the black foliage and the blue sky: a child. Native, Mayan stock. Huaxtec, probably, judging from his build and facial characteristics. A resident of the Quintano Roo region, most likely.

"Are you archaeologists?" she asked.

"We are assassins," the old one said.

That was it. Even valium wouldn't help now.

"What'd she start screaming for?" Remo shouted above the woman's wailing.

"Because she is female," Chiun said.

"Is she hurt?" Remo quickly pulled her out

through the opening, prodding her ribs and limbs. The screaming continued unabated. "Do you think she's in pain?"

"Who can say?" Chiun said, shrugging. "Women always feel pain, whether it exists or not."

"Let's get her over here, in the shade." Remo pulled her under a tree. "Now calm down, lady. You're all right."

Dr. Drake stopped screaming abruptly and looked up at him. "You're going to kill me, I suppose," she said.

Remo looked over to Chiun, then back at the woman. She was beautiful, lean and tall, with green eyes and blonde hair pulled up into an unkempt knot. It was the kind of thick Nordic hair that, under better circumstances, would be spilling over bare shoulders and onto her firm, big breasts between expensive sheets. A classy woman, lots of style. But nuts.

"Now, would you mind telling me why I'd go to the trouble of saving your life if I wanted to kill you?" Remo asked, exasperated.

"He said you were assassins," she said, looking warily at Chiun.

"That is true," Chiun said. "But it is not the honor of everyone to be assassinated by us. Most are unworthy of our talents. Especially foolish females who want to be rescued by machines."

She sat up, flushing. "Look, I was only saying—"

"The next time your life is in danger, we will send you a tractor."

"You two are impossible," she said hotly. "The fact of the matter is—"

"She's all right," Remo said.

"I am talking to you, mister," the woman spat.

"Remo. The name's Remo. This is Chiun. The kid's name is Po. Now introduce yourself like a civilized person, or we're going to leave you right here."

Her eyes flashed. Her mouth opened, ready for assault. But Remo had already turned away. "I'm Elizabeth Drake," she said haughtily.

Remo smiled. "Nice to meet you, Lizzie."

"It's Elizabeth. You may call me Dr. Drake. I'm an archaeologist."

"Oh, yeah. I heard the name. You and your buddy were digging around this place."

"Dr. Diehl?" she asked excitedly. "He's alive?"

"He's alive. It looks like you two are the only ones who made it out of here." He walked over to the wreckage of the Red Cross helicopter and surveyed the damage. No survivors. None on the ground outside the temple, either. The bodies lying beneath and around the fallen rocks were in an advanced state of decomposition. Some of them still showed evidence of strange wounds, huge holes that seemed to have burned clear through their targets.

Diehl was right, Remo thought. The weapons were lasers. He had seen that for himself. And they had attacked the Temple of Magic.

But who had provided the weapons in the first place? It was hard to believe, but somewhere in the middle of one of the most dense, primitive jungles on earth was—*had to be*—an arsenal of weapons more advanced than any produced by the United States. Advanced, and yet as fragile as spun glass.

Except for the wounds on some of the dead, there was no indication that the group had been attacked by any civilized agents of war. Maybe he would have more luck inside. He began to work at the rocks blocking the entrance. Most of the work had already been done while he and Chiun were seeking a way to the barracuda who permitted herself to be called Dr. Drake.

The inside of the temple was cool and dry in contrast to the sweltering humidity outside. Good, he thought as he dragged the lifeless bodies out into the open. He wasn't looking forward to the prospect of shoveling rotting flesh. These bodies carried the same wounds—gaping, penetrating, inflicted by laser weapons. Except for the archaeologists Elizabeth Drake had identified, they were all Indians, either from the dig's crew or the Lost Tribes. No Russians here.

Remo searched the interior of the temple. What was he looking for? Other weapons, maybe? A scrap of paper, a piece of fabric . . . anything that would tie the laser attack to someone other than the spear-carrying natives.

But there was nothing. Scattered among the debris on the floor were a few urns and pots. He picked one up and upturned it. Nothing but a fine fall of limestone came out. He tossed it into a corner.

"What are you doing?" Lizzie shrieked. She picked up the pot and cradled it in her arms like a baby. "Don't you know how valuable these things are? It's remarkable that they've even survived the earthquake." She snatched a piece of broken pottery from Remo's hands. "Don't touch these, you monster," she whispered hoarsely.

"It's only a broken piece of clay," Remo explained.

"For your information, this broken piece of clay is more than five thousand years old." She thrust it under Chiun's nose.

"I do not care for modern art," the old man said blandly.

Remo could see the cords standing up around the archaeologist's neck. "Loosen up, Lizzie," he said gently.

"Don't condescend to me!" she stormed.

"Okay, okay. I'm sorry about the pot. It just looked like a pot to me. It didn't look important."

"Not important?" she asked incredulously. She closed her eyes in mock despair. "Look. Maybe I ought to explain something. The branch of archaeology I specialize in is ancient Mayan civilization. I've been studying it for sixteen years, teaching, reading, writing about it. I've spent most of my adult life in this part of the world, where the Mayans originated. And yet I know next to nothing about them. No one does. The ancient Maya are a mystery that's baffled scholars for centuries. All we know about them is what we've been able to piece together from carved stones and ruins of buildings and broken pots, like the one you didn't think was important."

"I get the picture," Remo said wearily. He was tired of being lectured to, especially by someone whose life he just saved.

"No you don't," she persisted. "That's what I'm trying to explain to you. The Mayan civilization leaped, historically speaking, in a single, unexplained bound, from a primitive agrarian society to a complex system of cities that fostered art, sculpture, higher mathematics, advanced astronomy, a 360-day calendar, a complex writing system, and the concept of zero. In other words, they went from root farmers to scientific wizards almost instantaneously."

"What do you guys call instantaneous? A thousand years?"

"Try one day," Lizzie said.

Even Chiun looked up. "What was the day?" he asked.

Remo smiled. "She didn't mean one *particular* day, Chiun."

"Oh, yes I did," Lizzie said. "The day was August 11, 3114 B.C."

"How do you know that?"

"The date is written in nearly every major piece of Mayan writing discovered. That one date. It's in tombs, on walls, on the *stelae* monuments the Mayans cut from stone to record other events—everything. It's the beginning of time as the Maya knew it."

She ran her finger along the rim of the pot in her hand. "Something happened on that date fifty centuries ago," she said, almost to herself. "Something so monumental that it catapulted the Maya from the stone age into the future."

"Doesn't it say in these writings you've found?" Remo asked.

"No. It's always used as a reference, the way we use A.D. and B.C. Apparently what happened was so important that future generations just assumed everyone knew what the landmark event was. The earliest known Mayan structure ever uncovered was a ceremonial center at Cuello in northern Belize, dating to 2500 B.C. But that was just an empty room with a stone altar. Buildings don't keep well in this climate. Anyway, that's still more than 600 years after the magic date of 3114, B.C."

"So you still don't know anything," Remo said.

"That's just it. We might have the answer right here. The first team of archaeologists to explore this temple found evidence dating it to 3,000 B.C. or earlier."

She paused, searching Remo's eyes for recognition, then gave up in an impatient sigh. "Don't you see? The Temple of Magic is the most ancient Mayan site ever discovered. Right here in these walls may be the answer to a riddle that's thousands of years old. *What happened*?"

The boy watched her. Then suddenly he spoke. "It was Kukulcan," he said.

She turned to him. "What?"

"My father told me in the Old Tongue," he

said meekly. "In the legends, the white god Kukulcan came to earth in a flaming chariot to build the world."

"Utter rot," Lizzie said. "A useless folk tale."

The boy shrank back. "Take it easy," Remo said. "He's just a kid."

"I am a scientist," Lizzie said, "not a mother telling bedtime stories. Those so-called harmless legends can lead to seriously erroneous thought that hinders the way of real progress. That particular story about Kukulcan, for example, has spurred hundreds of normally sane people to believe that the Mayans were given their knowledge by invading spacemen. *Spacemen*! Have you ever heard of such lunacy?"

Remo shrugged, trying to keep his patience. People who'd lived through an ordeal like Lizzie Drake's entombment in the fallen temple were entitled to a little crabbiness when the crisis passed, but she was beginning to get on his nerves, beautiful chest or not. "Let's change the subject," he said pleasantly. "Seen any good movies lately?"

The archaelogist reddened. "Whose idea was it anyway to send you down here instead of a decently educated team?" she said through clenched teeth. "The nerve. The greatest archaeological find in history, and I've got nobody except an ignorant child, the oldest man in the world, and a buffoon in a T-shirt!"

"Look, lady. For what it's worth, this buffoon just saved your life. Which, from what I can see of your sparkling personality and charm, wasn't worth a fart in a bottle to begin with."

She rolled her eyes and made disdaining clucking noises with her mouth.

"If you weren't a woman, I'd smack you," Remo said, realizing that he was shouting, but not caring.

"Go ahead," Lizzie shrilled. "Prove what a male chauvinist hotshot you are. You men, with your little peckers, your little fists—"

"Your little red ass," Remo muttered, walking toward her. She screamed.

"Stop, stop," Chiun said, clapping his hands over his ears. "This bickering is unbearable for one of my years. Shouting. Arguments. There can be no serenity where there is discord such as this. I must have tranquility in the twilight of my life." He smiled sweetly to Lizzie.

"Then go back to the old folks' home where you belong," she yelled.

Chiun's jaw clamped shut. "Remo, this woman," he whispered.

"Yeah, I know. She brings out the best in a guy, doesn't she?"

"Remo! Chiun!" Po shouted from the far corner of the temple. The corner was piled high with fallen rock. The boy's head peered out from an opening between them. "Come here. Look."

"This is no place for children's games," Lizzie said, passing Remo en route to the boy. "He might damage something. It's bad enough to have two grown-up fools in here, but a *child* . . ."

Remo followed her, step for step, speaking directly into her ear. "I've had just about all the lipping off I'm going to hear out of you," he began. "I know how to shut you up." He reached a hand toward her throat, then noticed that Chiun had disappeared between the rocks. Po waited at the entrance, beckoning. He entered into a narrow passageway between the rocks when Remo arrived.

"What is it?" Remo asked.

"This way," Chiun's voice echoed from within the rubble.

The passageway through the rocks was low. Remo got on his hands and knees and felt his way through the darkness.

"I'm not going in there," Lizzie called from outside the tunnel of fallen rock.

"Good," Remo said.

"But I'm alone out here," she shouted. "What if those maniacs with the guns come back?"

"Maybe they'll shoot you," Remo said. "Death is just another way to get peace and quiet."

His heart sank as he heard the scuffle of hands and feet behind him. "Watch. Now we'll all be trapped," Lizzie complained, her voice echoing around him like a bad odor. "Some rescuers."

"Here it is," Po said in the darkness.

Chiun answered, "Ah, yes."

Remo's eyes adjusted automatically to the darkness in the tunnel. At the end, he saw Chiun and the boy standing in front of what looked like a refrigerator.

"What's this?" he asked, touching its surface as he rose to full height. It cracked beneath his fingers.

The object was oval, about five feet high, and metal. Metal that crushed on contact. On its left side was a handle of some kind. "I think it's a door," Remo said. He reached for the handle, then jumped back in surprise when it was suddenly bathed in a circle of light.

The light jiggled. Remo whirled around.

"Flashlight," Lizzie said. "Naturally, I'm the only one who remembered to bring one."

"You are the only one with eyes so weak as to need one," Chiun said. He brushed Remo's hands away and opened the metal door. Remo, Lizzie, and the boy followed him into the chamber beyond.

Inside, the flashlight's bobbing circle illuminated a strange sight. It was an aisle, made of linoleum, it seemed, only glossier, sturdier. The ceiling of the structure was rounded, as if they were standing in a long tube, and made of the same material. Everything looked crisp and new except for the sides of the structure. Along the walls, for some reason not apparent to any of them, hung ghostly gray layers of thick, rotting cloth, as fragile as cobwebs.

Remo squeezed past Lizzie back to the oval door and pushed on its rim with the heel of his hand. It disintegrated under the moderate pressure. "This is the same metal the laser guns were made of," he said. "But the floor's plastic." He moved to the cobwebby hangings suspended from the ceiling. "And these things . . ."

"Don't touch anything!" Lizzie bellowed. "We don't know how old this is."

"Oh, come on," Remo said. "This metal isn't even rusted."

"Some of these temples contain tombs that are nearly airtight," Lizzie said huffily. "At Palenque, for example—"

"It's a plane of some kind," Remo interrupted. "It's got to be. The aisles, the airlock door, the . . ."

His eyes automatically followed the light from Lizzie's flashlight. It was quivering on the far end of the tubular structure they were standing in.

"God, what's *that*?" Lizzie whispered.

The light rested on still another door. But this one was round and made of hard white plastic. The surface it rested on was a sphere. A giant plastic ball.

"Don't tell me *that's* five thousand years old," Remo said.

"Oh, God. Not the spaceman theory. It can't be." Lizzie's hands shook as she walked toward the white globe. She opened the door.

The spheroid interior was heavily and uniformly padded with some kind of springy orange plastic. Six sets of seat belts dangled from the walls as if the pod were a ride at an amusement park, a luxurious, expensive version of the Tilt-A-Whirl.

Chiun and the boy explored the round, soft

chamber as Lizzie fingered the seatbelts. Could this have been the discovery that the first archaeological team had written to the university about—the thing that was so important that they dared not put it down on paper? The thing the naked tribesmen were willing to kill to protect?

Her mind was racing. She had not seen the vehicle when she first arrived at the Temple of Magic. Apparently a wall had been erected around it. The Mayans did that; it made sense. The temple within the temple.

"I'm going to take a look at the other end," Remo said.

Lizzie jumped out of her reverie. "I'll come with you." She stepped awkwardly out of the pod, following Remo down the smooth aisle.

"Get back," Remo said. His voice was quiet, imperative.

"Don't bully me," she said. "I'm the archaeologist. I have every right—"

"*Get back*!" He shoved her toward the pod. She fell, landing on her rump outside the open door.

"How dare you," she seethed. But the floor was moving beneath her, and she recognized the tremors. "Earthquake!"

"Get in there," Remo shouted, picking her up bodily and tossing her into the padded ball. "You'll be safer in there."

The floor heaved crazily. The shock propelled Remo backward, sending him crashing against the fragile, cobwebby hangings. His back struck something hard and plastic. A knob. No, a *switch*,

Remo thought. A plastic switch imbedded into some material that shattered like glass from the weight of his body.

The cloth in front of it exploded into dust. Outside, in the main chambers of the temple, more rocks were falling, crashing thunderously to earth.

"Hurry," Chiun said. He had picked the screaming woman off the floor and buckled her into one of the safety belts. The boy Po strapped himself in wordlessly.

A good kid, Remo thought, pulling himself with small, rapid steps toward the padded pod. He's keeping his head. Chiun was right about him. He'd been right about the girl, too. Pain in the ass from the word go. Without her, the two of them would have been able to get out into the open with the boy. He was small and kept himself still. But they'd never make it with a hysterical, screaming adult hampering every movement.

Another wave hit. Just outside the door, Remo flew off his feet again. Chiun's arm swept out to take hold of Remo's and pulled him inside the pod. He slammed the door closed.

The old man was standing in the center of the padded chamber, his minute movements keeping him in perfect balance as the woman and the boy jolted wildly beneath their belts.

Remo breathed deeply. The shaking was a lot less pronounced in the pod.

"What did I tell you?" Lizzie shrieked. "We're trapped. Just as I said."

"Score one for you," Remo said nastily.

"We're all going to die here," she moaned.

"For once, just shut up, okay? You're safer in here than anywhere else. We couldn't get outside now if . . . if . . ."

He glanced around the pod. Lizzie had stopped making noise and was staring at him in alarm. The boy, too, was looking up at him, open-mouthed. Remo heard himself speaking, but the voice was not his own. It was deep, dragging, hollow sounding. Slow, growing slower, like an old phonograph record winding down.

He looked to Chiun. The movement of turning his head seemed to take minutes. Chiun blinked, a long, lazy motion. Remo walked toward the door. He felt as if he were treading through molasses.

"Hold," came Chiun's voice, distorted and languid. "Do . . . not . . . open . . . it. . . ."

Lizzie screamed. The sound filled the pod like a balloon, encapsulated and faraway. Her face was contorted, the mouth twisting slowly, the planes of her flesh seeming to wave like a mirage.

Po, in slow motion, reached his thin arm out toward Chiun. The old Oriental clasped the child's hand and squeezed it.

Remo pressed his back against the padded wall. His vision was fading, the colors in front of him dissolving to gray, then black, until there was no light, nothing but the sound of breathing in the small room: Lizzie's loud and gasping, amplified and slow. The boy's panting, sounding like a rhythmic hiss. Remo's own deep, soft intake, ringing through his ears like wind. And Chiun the Master's, barely audible.

Chapter Six

When Remo came to, the earthquake had stopped and Chiun was standing in front of the pod's open door, his hand lightly touching its handle. The old man's face showed concern. "Come here, Remo," he said softly.

"What is it?" Lizzie groaned, unfastening the seat belt around her waist. The boy blinked sleepily, as if he had just awakened from a nap.

"What the *hell*," Remo whispered as he stepped from the pod. The cobwebby gray hangings draped on either side of the aisle were replaced by bright woven cloth, stiff with gold and red paint, depicting primitive scenes of animals and children at play.

"These are *new*," Lizzie said, peering at the hangings.

Remo shook his head, bewildered. "But I wrecked two of them. They fell apart like they were made of powder. I saw it myself." He moved forward down the white plastic aisle of the craft, through the vehicle's airlock door, past a new wall recently erected around the sides of the door.

Beyond the wall was a chamber, intact, filled with extravagant artworks: Vases encrusted with turquoise and shell, gold ornaments in shapes of fanciful animals, boxes of jade and silver, filled with pearls and precious stones.

"It's magnificent," Lizzie whispered from behind him. "Perfect. The most perfect examples of Mayan art I've ever seen."

"Stay back," Remo said.

"What for? I'm as puzzled by this as you are. Why shouldn't I look?" she said petulantly, moving through the fabulous chamber. She stopped, frowning, near an eight-foot-high statue of a man, sculpted in the classic Mayan block manner except for the head, which had no features at all. Instead, sitting atop the figure's shoulders was a blank stone sphere.

"That's odd," she said. "There's no face." She turned from the statue and picked up an oval vase sitting on a pedestal near a doorway. "Absolutely priceless," she said, turning the vase in her hands.

A piercing scream broke the silence. Lizzie's vase dropped from her hands and shattered on the floor.

Remo and Chiun looked at one another. The sound was one they knew, because only one creature could produce it, and in only one circumstance: it was the scream of a man succumbing to violent death.

They searched the walls for an entrance. Remo found it, a short maze leading from the room of treasures into a third chamber. What lay inside it made his stomach churn.

A group of men, tall and slender and dark-haired, attired in fine robes woven with intricate patterns and gold thread, were clustered silently around a four-foot-high altar where a youth—a boy of sixteen or younger—lay. His arms and legs were bound with rope. His chest was laid open, its torn flesh still bright with new blood.

Behind the youth stood the most gloriously garbed personage of all, a man of aristocratic features and deep blue eyes that shone with the passion of a hunter after the kill. He was dressed in a gown of purest silver, and he wore a thick silver ornament on his head like a crown. His arms were heavy with bangles of jade and carved bone, and on his chest dangled a giant topaz on a silver chain.

In one upraised hand was a dagger, large and slick with dripping blood. In the other was the still-beating heart of the youth.

At the sight of the intruders, the finely robed men gasped and murmured among themselves. Only the one in the middle, the one holding the dying heart, remained silent. His eyes narrowed as he muttered something low and menacing in a language half fluid, half guttural, a language Remo had never heard before.

"What'd he say?" he asked Chiun, who knew the speech of most of the world.

The old man frowned. "I do not know," he said. "I have not heard this language before."

"I thought I picked out certain derivatives of local Mayan speech," Lizzie said excitedly. "Maybe it's some kind of cult, or—"

"It is the Old Tongue," the boy said softly.

They all turned to look at him. "The Old Tongue?" Remo asked.

"The language of my ancestors," Po said, his eyes fixed on the tall man covered with blood. "He told us to leave."

"Gladly," Chiun said.

The man spoke again, pointing at Remo and Chiun. His voice was deep and resonant, his face cruel.

"What was that?" Remo asked. But the boy didn't answer. Instead, he stepped forward, his chin jutting, his face flushed, and shouted something at the man.

As he spoke, the other members of the group around the bloody table looked uncertainly at one another, then fixedly at Remo and Chiun. At one point, the leader of the group opened his mouth to speak, but the boy silenced him with a fresh torrent of the strange-sounding words, gesturing to the sky, then pointing again at Remo and Chiun. His childish voice took on a peculiar air of command as he spoke, standing still, his posture erect, his voice clear. When he was finished, the men standing around the table lowered their eyes. The boy snapped out another command, and they sank to their knees, chanting something in unison.

Only the central figure remained standing, the man in the splendid robes whose topaz amulet glinted with reflected blood. He stared at Po, his eyes as cold as the dagger still in his hand.

Po did not speak again, and his eyes never left the man's. Then, after what seemed like hours, the tall man laid down the stilled heart and the dagger, nodded once curtly, and strode out.

"Come," the boy said. "He is taking us to his king."

"That was some showdown," Remo said, following him through the temple toward the entrance. "What was going on back there? Should we have done something?"

"No," Po said. "It was a sacrifice. That is their way. The man is a priest." He added, "But I do not trust him.

"He didn't look like he was crazy about you, either," Remo said. "How'd you talk him into taking us out of here?"

"I told him the truth," Po said.

"Oh? You mean that we got stuck in an earthquake and somehow ended up in the wrong temple? He bought that?"

"Well, not exactly the truth," the boy said. "I told him that we fell to earth in a flaming chariot."

"Oh, good," Remo said. "Something believable."

"And that he should be prepared to deal with the great god Kukulcan and his son."

Chiun beamed. "I knew there was something I liked about this boy," he said.

Outside the temple, the view that greeted them was a shock. The jungle brush that had all but obliterated the sunlight had been cleared. In its place was a thriving city of baked clay and cement and stone buildings, some of which were of immense proportions.

A row of merchants in cloth covered stalls shouted to passersby, displaying a wide variety of wares: obsidian blades; tobacco in large, dried leaves; blocks of white rock salt; dried fish; stacks of dishes and pottery; masks decorated with fine colored feathers and bright paint; metal incense burners; flint; canes and staves; jade and jewelry.

Dazed, Lizzie exlained some of the more unusual items in the stalls as they passed by. A shop displaying nothing but white spikes was, she said, the place to buy stingray spines.

"They used to be used for bloodletting," she said, adding lamely, "Maybe they still do. Somewhere . . ."

She was beginning to shake. "Calm down," Remo said. "We'll find out where we are soon enough."

"But we *didn't move*!" she protested.

"We don't know that," Remo said reasonably. "Everything went crazy once the earthquake hit. We might have moved." He corrected himself. "We had to have moved. We wouldn't be here if we hadn't."

"But the temple—"

"Save the questions for when we get where we're going," Remo snapped. He knew it didn't make sense that they had left in a vehicle that was buried inside a temple of rock and emerged inside another man-made structure, but Lizzie's whining complaints didn't help make things any clearer. He needed time to think.

First, he would see whoever was in charge of the murderous strangers whose city he was in. He would ask questions; he would think. And then he might be able to piece things together.

They passed a stall filled with small clay animal figurines. The merchant picked up a small, brightly colored clay bird and demonstrated its use by blowing into its tail. As the air rushed through, he worked his fingers over a series of holes on the bird's back. A pretty melody came out.

"Toys," Lizzie said distractedly, plucking at her trousers. The women who walked curiously past them were dressed in bright cotton togas, the folds of the garments flowing from clasps at one shoulder. The men wore little more than strips of cloth wound between their legs. Both sexes sported elaborate hairstyles, their long black hair twisted on top of their heads and studded with ornaments. No one seemed particularly surprised at the attire of the little group.

"This is some kind of trade center," Lizzie said.

"Yeah. They must be used to tourists," Remo said.

He wasn't going to waste time wondering what had happened. Somehow, the spherical pod they had been in had transported them to another place. Where was anybody's guess. But they were alive, and they were unharmed, and in the teachings of Sinanju, that was the whole game.

A pretty woman walking a spider monkey on a leash sauntered in front of him, clacking something in her palm. She smiled. Remo smiled back. Well, that's a good sign, he thought. At least the natives are friendly.

She walked along beside him for a while. Then, with a sly look, she opened her hand. In it were a half-dozen hard, brown beans.

"Beans?" Remo asked.

The girl smiled.

"Strange customs," Remo mumbled, nodding and smiling.

She held the beans in front of him, jerking her head upward in a question.

"Uh—no thanks, I've just had lunch," Remo said gallantly.

The woman frowned, looking hurt. She thrust out her breasts to him.

"Hey, it's nothing personal," he said. "It's just that beans don't agree with me. Especially raw ones. Give me gas pockets. You know how rough those can be."

She blinked, uncomprehending.

"Oh, all right," Remo said, popping one of the beans into his mouth. "There. Thanks. Nothing hits the spot like a good bean or two, I always say."

The woman stepped back a pace, looking at the remaining beans in her hand, and then at Remo. Her face carried an expression of utter astonishment. Then she drew back her hand and slapped Remo roundly across the face, propelling the monkey forward. The monkey bit him in the leg.

"Hey, what was that for?" Remo shouted after the woman, who pranced away indignantly. "All I did was eat one of her stupid beans."

Lizzie pulled her gaze away from the amazing sights of the town and stared at Remo. "Beans?" she asked.

"Yeah, beans. The bean lady of the Twilight Zone," Remo said crankily.

"What did they taste like?"

Remo thought a moment. "Chocolate," he said finally. "It was a chocolate bean. What difference does that make?"

"Chocolate," Lizzie whispered, her face ashen. "A cacao bean."

"Listen, if you're hungry, go find your own bean. I'm not getting slugged again."

"That woman was a prostitute. She wanted you to pay her in beans."

Remo's eyebrows rose. "Sounds like pretty cheap rates," he said.

"For now. Not for five thousand years ago."

"Again with the museum lectures," Remo said despairingly.

Lizzie continued, undaunted. "During the third millennium B.C., cacao beans were used as currency. They were the medium of exchange. There's even evidence that there were counterfeiters who filled bean skins with dirt."

"Okay, Lizzie," Remo said wearily. "I promise

you that while I'm here I won't go into the funny bean business."

"Don't you know what I'm saying?" she shrieked. "The clothes here. The buildings. *Sting ray spines*, for God's sake. Everything points to it. Even the temple."

Feeling a shiver run down the back of his neck, Remo turned to look at the building where they had left the curious round plastic pod. In the place of the moss-covered ruin was a magnificent pyramidal edifice, six stories tall, tiered and decorated in bright colors.

"Everything points to what?" Remo said cautiously.

"You know perfectly well," she said softly. "This is not another place. *It's another time.*"

Stunned, Remo walked quickly to the boy and took him by the shoulders. "Po, I want you to ask that priest where we are," he said. "And *when.*"

Po spoke to the priest. After a haughty silence, the tall man answered.

"The name of the place is Yaxbenhaltun," the boy reported.

"And the date?"

"He says it is nine *tun*, eighteen *uinal.*"

"What?"

The boy shrugged.

"The time measurement the ancient Mayans used," Lizzie said. "A *tun* is a year. A *uinal* is a period of twenty days. This present moment is roughly ten years after the event of 3114 B.C.," she said, her voice hushed with excitement.

"Are you crazy?" Remo shouted, appalled.

"You're saying that we've *gone back in time*. Do you know how ridiculous that sounds? How impossible?"

Chiun, who had kept silent since their confrontation with the priest, spoke. "Nothing is impossible," he said softly.

For a moment, all four of them stood staring at the sparkling new temple in the middle of a thriving city.

A city that had been dead since the time of the Pharaohs.

Chapter Seven

They were led to a huge low building near the great wall separating the city from the farmland outside on the outskirts of the endless jungle. Like the temple, the wall was constructed of stones cemented by mortar and rubble and coated with bright white stucco. Orange tiles covered the vast roof, and a lush garden of tropical flowers outlined the fanciful walkways leading into the building's canopied entrances.

In the stone foyer was a statue like the one in the temple, depicting the figure of a man topped by a blank sphere in place of a head. The priest led them silently past the bronze-colored guards dressed in white loincloths, their heads and spears festooned with ornamental quetzal feathers, up an elegant curving staircase of stone. They walked through a long hallway whose walls were brightly painted with scenes of men playing ball. Finally they entered a large airy room filled with priceless pottery encrusted with gems. Its high ceiling was decorated with painted moldings and rounded archways leading to adjacent rooms.

In the center of the main room where they stood were three statues. Two smaller plaster figures, around six feet tall, flanked a larger central statue. The central figure was, again, the ever-present man whose head was a blank sphere.

"I recognize the two smaller ones," Lizzie said. "The one on the left is Ah Kin, the Mayan God of Light, and that's Ah Chac, the Rain God, on the right. But I still can't figure out the one in the middle. That statue seems to be everywhere, and yet I've never seen one unearthed."

"I guess he's some kind of local big deal," Remo said distractedly. He couldn't care less about some bubble-headed statue. He walked over to Chiun, who was looking serenely out one of the room's big windows.

Outside, past the city's walls, were small thatched-roof houses made of poles and stucco. Women crouched in the dirt courtyards around the rough dwellings, weaving on hip looms and carrying loaves of bread to big stone ovens. Beyond them were the farms, the earth terraced and stepped to preserve the soil from erosion. Tall corn waved gently in the breeze, and red dots of tomatoes and peppers brightened the peaceful landscape in front of the jungle.

"This is a good time," Chiun said.

"How can you say that?" Remo snapped.

"We're trapped sometime in prehistory. There isn't even a phone here."

The old Oriental shrugged. "A man is trapped only by the limitations of his mind," he said.

"Great. I'll remember that while I'm inventing the wheel."

"Don't be foolish, Remo. This is a civilized place. Look at it. There is agriculture here, and art, and peace. There are no guns or cars or radios growing out of the necks of knife-wielding dolts."

"I can't believe it," Remo said. "You don't care. You really don't care whether we get home or not, do you?"

"Be patient, my son. I do care. But I do not worry needlessly."

"Needlessly? We get thrown back in time by some fluke—"

Chiun held up a restraining finger. "No, not a fluke. We are here because it is somewhere decreed that we must be here. When it is no longer necessary for us to be here, we will leave. When it is time. Not before."

Remo realized that it was useless to talk to the old man. Chiun was off on one of his metaphysical tirades, and nothing was going to change his mind until he decided it was time. Wonderful. He would have to figure out how to get out of this mess by himself.

"Po," he shouted to the boy who was touring the other rooms. "What's supposed to happen now?"

The boy limped into the doorway. "The priest said we are to meet the king here."

"I've got it," Lizzie said, running up to him.

"What?"

She pulled him in front of the three statues. "The only god more important to the Mayans than Ah Kin and Ah Chac was Kukulcan, the white god."

Remo rolled his eyes. "Terrific, Lizzie. I'm glad to hear it. Chalk one up for Whitey."

"You know, it's always been a mystery why the Mayans would worship a white god. Kukulcan's name is found in inscriptions long before the first Spanish invasion in the fifteen hundreds. The prevailing theory is that the Mayans borrowed the god from the Mexican deity Quezalcoatl, but those connections were never really proven, either." She chewed at her fingernails, her eyes glazed. "Only it can't be Kukulcan. At least not the Kukulcan I've seen."

"Huh? What are you talking about?" Remo said, annoyed. He pried her fingers off his arm.

"The statue. Kukulcan is always shown as a stylized man covered with snakes and feathers."

"Oh, so what?" Remo snapped. "Who gives a crap what he's wearing?"

"But he's wearing a bubble," Lizzie persisted.

Remo flushed. "I don't care if he's wearing a goddamned G-string. Will you lay off? For your information, we've got other problems. Like how the hell to get out of this time warp."

"For your information, I'm telling you," Lizzie said hotly.

"How to get out of here?'

"How we got in here. That's a start."

"I know how we got here. It was something in that pod we were in. I hit something when the earthquake started. There was a reaction."

"That's what I'm saying. The statue's wearing a *bubble.* A spacesuit. What we're looking at is some kind of interplanetary spaceman who could travel through time."

Remo looked at her, dumbfounded. "You're getting worse by the minute," he said at last.

"It's the only possibility. The great leap of the Mayans. A *spaceman.* The spaceman theory was right. I suspected it as soon as I saw the pod."

A low, ringing, melodious note sounded outside the doorway leading into the hall.

"What was that?" Lizzie said, shocked out of her thoughts.

"Sounded like a gong," Remo said. He went forward to check. As he reached the doorway, a stony-faced man in a loincloth entered, blocking his way. Behind the man came another, followed by four more, walking to the accompaniment of beating drums and flutes.

Chiun turned from the window. The men fell into two rows on either side of the doorway and knelt. Chiun smiled beatifically.

"Really, there is no need for such ceremony," he said indulgently.

"I don't think it's for us," Remo said.

The music stopped. A second gong sounded. The tall priest who had guided them into the building walked in. He stared straight ahead, except for a brief, cold glance at the boy. He spoke something, then turned toward the doorway and bowed.

"The king," the boy whispered.

Six more dark men—slaves, Remo guessed—shuffled in, eyes lowered, carrying a covered sedan chair on their shoulders. The cloth of the litter was of gold studded with large turquoises. When the slaves set the chair down, they fell immediately to their knees facing the priest. Two of them reached out their arms and pulled back the shimmering curtains.

A hand, old and withered and trembling, reached out from the litter. The priest took it in his own and, still kneeling, helped the old man from his seat.

The king, his white hair pulled back into a knot on top of his head, was clearly a sick man. The flesh of his face sagged, and his sunken chest shook with the force of deep, hacking coughs. He spoke to the priest, the words barely audible.

The priest stood, stepping away deferentially from the old man, who spread his frail arms wide.

He gestured as he spoke, nodding to Remo and Chiun, and pointed to the statue of the bubble-headed man.

"He says welcome, children of Kukulcan," the boy said.

The priest glared at Po, but the king stepped forward and cupped the boy's face in his trembling hands. He asked a question, and the boy answered. The king looked over to Remo and Chiun in wonder, said something else, softly, and then was seized by an attack of coughing.

The priest spoke sharply to the boy before leading the old king back to the sedan chair. Before he sat, however, the king spoke again to the bewildered group. His expression was stricken. Then he let himself be covered in the litter and carried out.

"What was that about?" Remo said when the four strangers were alone again.

"It was confusing," the boy said. "He said that the prophecy has come to pass, and that he is prepared to keep his bargain."

"Bargain? What bargain?"

"I don't know. He called me the voice of the gods."

"That's us, I suppose," Remo said drily.

"There is to be a ceremony for you tomorrow morning at the volcano of Bocatan."

"Well, I suppose we can talk to him then," Remo said.

The priest again appeared in the doorway, fixing them all with his stony stare. Slowly he lifted his arms and clapped his hands. Then he backed away and was gone.

"Cheerful little scamp," Remo said, looking down the hall after him. "Hold on, troops. I think the USO is here."

Wooden flutes and tambourines sounded, filling the hall with strange music. Remo came back into the room, shaking his head. Behind him pranced musicians and servants bearing huge trays heaped with food. There were chilies, tomatoes, corn, squash, pumpkins, papaya, avocado, and loaves of breadnut, as well as the boiled carcasses of rabbit, iguana, and armadillo. One tray was heaped to overflowing with large rolled leaves, and on another were laid a dozen fish, which the servant identified as Xoc. There were silver pitchers of brown liquid giving off potent alcoholic fumes, and gold ones holding a murky white drink.

"This is balché," Po said, sniffing the brown drink. "It is a traditional drink made of fermented honey and tree bark. Very strong."

"I'll pass," Remo said. "What about this?" He leaned over the gold pitcher filled with white liquid. Instantly his vision blurred. Chiun pushed him aside and, using stern gestures, ordered every gold pitcher removed from the room.

"What was that stuff?" Remo asked.

"Did you not recognize the scent?" Chiun said. "It is an extract made from the white flowers we found in the fields. The sleeping flowers."

"Oh, I get it," Remo said. "Count Dracula's bedtime potion. Hey, what's that priest got against us, anyway?"

"He frightens me," the boy said.

Chiun came to them, pointing toward the doorway. "Look, Remo. Just what you like. Bare-breasted women."

Indeed, a line of slithering girls draped from the hip down in flowing fabric jingled into the room, bells dangling from their fluttering fingers.

"Now, this is more like it," Remo said.

The girls wove through the room, waving their long, unbound hair, their legs moving sinuously, eyes smiling. During their dance, they gathered up cushions into a luxurious banquette and led Remo and Chiun to them, seating them carefully.

"Did I not tell you it was a better time than the one we left?" Chiun said.

"It has its good points," Remo agreed, accepting a grape. "Who's that? The featured stripper?"

He pointed toward the doorway, where a quartet of burly slaves carried an obsidian disc on their shoulders. On top of the disc stood a very young girl, a child of no more than twelve. Wrapped from the neck down with shimmering white gauze and bedecked with heavy jewels, she stood like a statue as the slaves set her down in the center of the room. She remained there, motionless, her wide gray eyes frightened and transfixed.

"Hey, she's just a kid," Remo said. He called to Po, who was standing a few feet away, his mouth hanging open at the sight of her.

The boy didn't respond. Remo went over to him. "You all right?"

"She is the most beautiful creature I have ever seen," Po said.

Remo smiled. "There'll be others."

"No others," the boy said. "Ever."

It's all right, Remo thought. Let the kid have his dream girl. By the time they figured out how to leave this place, Po would be as happy as the rest of them to get out.

"Who is she?"

"Her name is Nata-Ah. I heard one of the servants talking about her. She is the king's granddaughter."

"Why's she just standing there? She shy or something?"

"She is not permitted to speak. She is here so that we may look on her beauty."

"Oh. Kind of like a painting, only living, right?"

The boy didn't hear him. His thoughts were on the girl standing in the middle of the room, a white angel surrounded by shapes without form, sound without sense. She was, the boy knew, the reason he had not died with the rest of his family, the reason he had survived the massacres of the Lost Tribes. She was what had awaited him at his journey's end.

The girl, Nata-Ah, granddaughter of the king, child of the forgotten centuries, was his destiny.

Chapter Eight

The water was steaming and fragrant with infusions of herbs. Remo, naked, allowed the beautiful bath girls to dry and oil him on one of the long benches of the tiled palace bathhouse. Chiun, draped in a white toga, occupied a small corner of the Olympic-sized pool, slapping away the hands that came to tend to him.

"Get away. Can the Master of Sinanju not expect even a modicum of privacy in this place?"

"I thought you liked it here."

"I like motel bathrooms better. Make them go away."

Remo sighed. "Okay, ladies, it's a wrap," he said, gesturing them out. They left, giggling.

"When is this dumb ceremony, anyway?" Remo asked.

"Soon. Dress yourself. You have no shame."

Remo slipped into his trousers. "Can't you go without me? I want to check out that—whatever it was that we came here in."

"You will attend," Chiun said. "While we are here, we follow the custom of our hosts. Who knows? Perhaps the king has need of the Master of Sinanju's skills. Think diplomatically, Remo."

"I'm trying to get us out of here," Remo protested.

"Try after the ceremony."

There was a solemn knock at the bamboo bathhouse door, sending echoes reverberating. It creaked open and Po walked in. He was covered by a magnificent robe, and carried two others. "These are for you," he said. "For the ceremony. The king sent them. Dr. Lizzie is already dressed."

"Will you look at these?" Remo said, running his hand over the jeweled garments.

Chiun stepped out of the water and passed an overly casual glance over the robes. "Not as good as those made in Sinanju," he said.

"Yours has lumps of gold stuck on the front," Remo said, holding up the small robe encrusted with glittering metal.

"Gold? Real gold?"

"See for yourself."

"Ah," he said, snatching it away from Remo. "Mine is much finer than yours. I told you these were civilized people." He compared the two robes. "But then, yours has emeralds in it." A frown crossed his face.

"Use it for a turban," Remo said. "I'm going the way I am."

"You cannot. This is high ceremony."

"I don't care if it's Halloween. I plan to get out

of here, and I'm not going back dressed as the Grand Poobah."

Remo stood in chinos and a black T-shirt atop the smoldering rim of the sacred volcano Bocatan while the nobles assembled. Clad in a lovely robe, Lizzie was curiously silent, taking in the scene around her. Chiun, beaming, glittered like a gem beside Remo. "Very wise choice, wearing your own clothes," he whispered. "Where is the king? Do you think he will be perturbed that I have formed your robe into a cape?"

"He was in such bad shape, I don't think he'll have much on his mind except living for the next twenty minutes. I think I see the litter down there."

Slowly, with awesome precision, the slaves made their careful way up the mountain with the covered sedan chair. Behind the king's litter was another, of purest white, for the girl, Nata-Ah. Behind them both, at the end of the procession, walked the priest.

He first helped the king from his chair, then returned for Nata-Ah. The girl was pale and apprehensive, her eyes glassy. She stepped to the rim of the volcano with faltering steps and took her place between her grandfather and the priest, opposite Remo and the others. Her head was high, the long unbound black hair shining with youth.

The priest began to speak. His voice was low, his words clear and carrying. As he spoke, the girl's chin quivered. The king bowed his head.

"What's going on?" Remo whispered to the boy, who frowned uncomprehendingly.

"It is—it cannot be," Po said, listening to the priest. Then his eyes widened. "He is going to sacrifice the girl!" he shouted. "The evil one is going to give Nata-Ah to the volcano."

He ran, limping, to the other side of the rim. "You will not do this thing!" he screamed, thrusting both of his small fists into the priest's chest.

The priest staggered backward. The king and the other nobles murmured in shocked dismay. Nata-Ah herself stood rigid, her eyes ablaze and fixed on the small lame boy who had dared to object to her death.

In one motion, the priest grabbed the boy's arms and whirled him around. "This opportunity will not be wasted, little one," he muttered in the Old Tongue. Only Po heard him. Only Po knew that the tall man was pushing him backward, toward the rim of the sacred fire mountain Bocatan to create an accident that would cost the boy his life.

"You will not stop me," the Priest said, edging the boy closer to the smoldering edge. "My work is too important. Your powers are as nothing compared with mine. Go to your death, small voice of the false gods. Your destiny shall not be fulfilled." With that, he placed his foot behind the boy's bad leg and toppled him, screaming, over the side.

In the fraction of a second, a blur beginning on the far side of the volcano's rim shot downward in a diagonal. It was so fast that to the onlookers the motion seemed to be a flash of lightning or a streak of smoke. Gasps went up. Eyes turned skyward. Only Chiun remained calm, observing, evaluating the movement inside the volcano. Remo was gone.

He had leaped in a spinning series of somersaults from the volcano's rim to project himself diagonally across the thirty-foot opening to meet the exact spot the boy had reached during his descent toward the bubbling red lava below.

Still in his spinning motion, Remo jammed his shoulder into the pliable inner wall of the volcano and set his feet behind him so that he appeared to be floating alongside the wall. At this height the molten rock was warm but not hot—the temperature of sand on a hot day. The holds of his shoulder and his feet left both his arms free. Then reaching out, careful not to dislodge his shoulder grip, he grabbed the fabric of the boy's robe and pulled him toward his own body.

Po's eyes were dark and still, the pupils shrunken in shock. "Take it easy, kid," Remo said, wrapping the boy's limp arms around his neck. "You've got to hang on now. That's all. Just hang on, okay?"

The boy's head turned slowly. When his eyes met Remo's, a flicker of recognition came into them. He nodded once, and Remo felt the thin arms grip tightly.

"That's good. Just hang on. I'll do the rest." He inched up the wall slowly, first moving one foot upward behind him, then the other, then sliding his shoulder up, pressing it into the wall of the volcano, creating a deep groove as he went. With each movement, smooth and continous with the last, he made compensations for the minute shift in weight caused by the boy's breathing.

It was the reverse of climbing up a sheer surface, a skill Remo had mastered years ago. The balance shifted with the weight and moved the body upward and in, toward the surface. To outsiders, wall climbing seemed a feat of magic, but in the training of Sinanju, it was elementary.

This was the same procedure, only his back was against the wall instead of his chest, his weight pressing into the surface, pushing it upward. When Remo neared the rim of the opening, he slid his two arms up behind him and clasped the edge. Then, propelling himself out of position, he spun in the air and landed feet first in his former position beside Chiun. The boy was on his feet, too, although the movements that had loosened his grip on Remo and thrown him through the air had happened too fast for him to follow.

He could only stare at the thin man with the thick wrists along with the others who stared, the king and the priest and the nobles. Then he turned to face Nata-Ah. The girl was watching him, her body tense. Her eyes melted, and she smiled. For a moment, the boy wished it would all happen again.

The king looked to the priest, his old eyes

hard as flint. He rasped out a harsh command. There was no other sound. The priest stood still, looking for an instant as if he would speak. Instead, he turned on his heel and descended down the mountain. No one spoke until the figure of the priest grew small on the bare footpath on the far side of the volcano. He walked away from the city, into the depths of the jungle.

The old king bowed to Remo and then to Chiun.

"No," the Oriental said, pulling the king to his feet. "Tell him that my son and I are not his gods."

"But you *are*," the boy protested. "Your magic powers—"

"That is strength and discipline and training. But not magic," Chiun said. "Tell the king that Chiun, the Master of Sinanju, and his apprentice stand before him. Not gods, but men like himself. Tell him."

Po did as he was told. The king stared at the strangers, obviously confused.

"Now tell him that we want to know what the hell's going on here," Remo said.

"The priest's name is Quintanodan," the king said in the safety of his throne room. He spoke haltingly, struggling for breath, as Po translated. "But the story begins long before the appearance of the priest. Ten years ago, the great white god Kukulcan descended into this valley in his flaming chariot to bring to my kingdom enlightenment and prosperity. I ruled then, as I rule now. Behind me in succession was my only son, Pachenque, who was prepared to take my place as king of the most advanced empire on earth. Pachenque's wife had borne only one child, the girl Nata-Ah, but she was young, and expected to bear many sons.

"Although Kukulcan spoke little, he was a wise and just god. He and his divine servants who had come to earth with him gave us drawings to help us plow our fields and plant our crops. He showed us how to make roads and construct buildings that will last for a thousand years. He taught my people to read the stars. He gave us the gift of numbers. He cured the sick with his magic, then gave the healing magic to others to cure. All we now have, we owe to Kukulcan."

"This—god," Remo said, "was actually here? I mean, alive?"

The king nodded. "That is his likeness." He gestured toward the statue of the man with the blank sphere for a head.

"Where did he come from?" Lizzie asked.

"I do not know. I cannot speak the language of the gods. But he showered my people with his blessings. He even drove the evil Olmec away from our land, past the fire mountain Bocatan, deep into the caves of death, into Xibalba, where lives the god of the dead. Kukulcan vanquished them with his magic spears of fire."

"Uh—didn't you think it was strange for a god to touch down in the middle of your city?" Remo said.

The king blinked. "But it was the prophecy. We expected the god, and Kukulcan came."

"What prophecy?"

The most ancient of the sacred writings. Long ago, it was spoken that a great god would come to guide the ruler of the kingdom of Yaxbenhaltun to greatness over all other peoples. I was that ruler. This is the kingdom of the prophecies."

"So the prophecies came true," Lizzie said.

"Not all. There is more. The sacred writings said that the god would visit, but that the voice of the gods would lead us to even greater heights, to a glory unimaginable in the eyes of mortal men."

Remo looked to Chiun, who nodded to the king in mute understanding.

"Then the calamity happened. Kukulcan disappeared. Or deserted us. I did not—I still do not know how I offended the good god, but he left with his friends one day, past the fire mountain Bocatan, into the Forbidden Fields, and was lost to us forever."

"Toward the Olmec caves?" Remo asked.

"Yes, but the Olmec could not have killed Kukulcan and his servants."

"Why not?"

"The gods are invincible. The cave dwellers could not vanquish them. We waited for his return. We erected a temple around his flaming chariot and prayed to all the gods for his return, but he did not come. Instead, we found only misfortune. The Olmec attacked again, setting fire to my palace and killing Pachenque, my only son. Now there is only Nata-Ah left to rule after I am gone."

"And Quintanodan the priest?" Chiun asked.

"He was a wandering holy man, possessed of the Sight. Quintanodan promised to bring back the power of Kukulcan to my kingdom in exchange for one service: that, on the return of the god, I should sacrifice my granddaughter Nata-Ah to the fire mountain Bocatan."

"And you thought we were the returning gods," Remo said.

"For Kukulcan, I would sacrifice the last of my dynasty," the old king said with dignity. "But at the fire mountain I saw that you did not wish this sacrifice. I knew then that Quintanodan was still my enemy."

"Still?"

"He is Olmec," the king said. "I have known for many years. But I said nothing, because without the power of Kukulcan I do not wish to wage war with the Olmec, who are sly and murderous and will burn my city and kill its women and children. I retained the priest, keeping spies secretly trained on him and avoiding any talk of important matters in his presence. Since he has been with me, the Olmec have not attacked."

"But if he was your enemy, why did you listen to him?"

"I am a foolish old man," the king said. "I thought that perhaps, after all the years I have given him shelter and position, he would see the good of my people and come to be loyal to me.

But I know now that he wished only to kill my only successor and end my rule in Yaxbenhaltun so that the Olmec warriors could attack and conquer my people without resistance."

"Why did he try to kill Po?"

"Because I called him the voice of the gods. In the prophecy, the voice of the gods is to lead my kingdom to greatness. By pretending to recognize the lame boy as that voice, I forced Quintanodan to show his true nature. Now that I have banished him, the priest will return to his people to wage war on my kingdom."

"Then why did you let him go?" Remo asked. "You could have had the priest killed on the volcano."

"For two reasons," the king said. "The first is because this is a holy day. Ten years ago did Kukulcan appear from the sky in his flaming chariot. On this day every year, it is forbidden to kill in anger. I banished Quintanodan to the land of the dead, to return to the tribe of jackals that spawned him."

"But why? You said yourself he'll organize an attack."

The king shook his head. "I have told you there were two reasons why I dismissed Quintanodan. I saw what you did today, how you rescued the boy from the gaping mouth of Bocatan."

"So?"

"You are my second reason," the king said. "When I saw you fly into the depths of the fire mountain and return with the boy unharmed, I knew that the gods had returned. The prophecy is come to pass."

"But we're not gods," Remo explained.

The king's eyes sparkled. "Perhaps you are not Kukulcan. But you are worthy still. You will protect us from the Olmec."

The old man was seized with an attack of coughing.

"Stay with him," Remo said to Chiun. "I'm going to the spaceship."

Chapter Nine

While Chiun and the boy stayed with the king, Remo and Lizzie made for the small craft locked into the inner walls of the Temple of Magic.

"This was the panel," Remo said, going over to one of the brightly colored cloth squares lining the aisle of the ship. "I fell into it. It exploded into dust."

"I know," Lizzie said. "I saw it, too. That was another time, far in the future. The cloth is whole again now, because the incident of your falling into it hasn't happened yet. That's still thousands of years to come."

"It's hard to understand," Remo mumbled, pulling the cloth away. "It happened, I saw it happen, and now it didn't happen. Hey, here's something."

Behind the curtain was a metal console. The metal glowed with the same greenish tint as the fragile exterior of the ship. Remo pressed it with his fingers. It was harder than steel. He rushed to the ship's doorway and pounded on the metal. "It's holding," he said.

Lizzie did the same. "It must weaken with age," she said. "But it's got to be a powerful alloy to last all those years."

"Where did they come from?" Remo said slowly, walking back to the console. "This is no flaming chariot. Whoever Kukulcan was, he wasn't a god. This thing is some kind of transport." He ran his hand along the dark console. His fingers stumbled across something. "Lizzie, bring your flashlight over here."

The beam illuminated two small horizontal panels filled with numbers. One series read 0811 2032. The other, 0810 3104 (−).

"What's the minus for?" Lizzie asked.

"I don't know. But here's what I ran into." He pointed out a broken switch above the plates containing the digital series.

"Are you sure?" Lizzie asked skeptically. "There was an earthquake going on, you know."

"Yes, I'm sure," Remo mimicked.

"You don't have to get nasty. How could you tell you ran into a *switch*? It could have been anything. It all happened so fast—"

"I can feel these things," Remo said. "It was a switch. If it had been anything else, I would have known—oh, never mind. You wouldn't understand."

Lizzie trained the flashlight on his face. "Say, you're not exactly normal, are you?"

"What's that supposed to mean?"

"What you did at the volcano today. No

human being could have jumped into that hole, caught a falling body, and somersaulted out."

"I didn't somersault. I climbed out."

"How? That's molten lava in there."

"On my back," Remo said, pushing aside the flashlight.

"Where are you from, Remo?"

Remo sighed. "Newark, New Jersey. Now quit asking questions and give me the flashlight."

The sound of distant footsteps brought him to attention. "Turn that off," he whispered. "Someone's coming." He led her down the darkened aisle of the craft.

"See what I mean? I don't hear anything," Lizzie said.

"That's because you're always talking. Shut up for once, will you?" They crouched down.

A young man with an *ocote* torch entered alone and went straight for the panel covering the digital sequences. Remo widened his pupils to allow for the darkness and focused on the man's hands. They were touching the sequences, somehow altering the numbers. The process took less than a minute. When he was finished, the young man turned and left without disturbing anything else in the ship.

"What'd he do?" Remo mumbled, scanning the digital panels again and again. "0811 2032," he read. "0811 3104 minus. Minus. What the hell does minus mean?"

"Wait a second," Lizzie said. "Read that again."

"What? The numbers? Can't you see them? You're the one with the flashlight."

"I want to *hear* them."

Remo sighed. "All right. "Oh eight, eleven, twenty thirty-two. Oh eight, eleven, thirty-one oh—"

"Four," Lizzie finished breathlessly. "Thirty-one oh four."

"Minus."

"Exactly." Her eyes glinted. "It's staggering. This is going to make me the foremost authority on Mayan history in the world. The great Dr. Diehl himself is going to take courses from me."

"Before you write your Nobel Prize acceptance speech, would you mind telling me what is exactly?"

She looked up at him. "Look," she said, pointing to the numbers. "These are *dates*. Eight, eleven, 2032. August 11, in the year 2032, obviously the present day for the time travelers—the day when their spaceship crashed."

"And the other one?"

"The king said that today is ten years to the day from the time Kukulcan came. Remember that we're back in time, far back. The minus stands for B.C. It has to. That man came in here to change the date from 8/10 to 8/11. It's August 11, 3104 B.C. Ten years to the day when Kukulcan first came here in 3114. The magic date. The beginning of time. That was *it*."

"Wait a minute," Remo said, making a face. "There are holes a mile wide in that. In the first place, how do these people know to move the years *backward* instead of ahead? They don't know they're living three thousand years before Christ."

"Kukulcan—or whoever the alien was—must have shown them how to do it. That's immaterial, anyway."

"Immaterial? I suppose it's immaterial that your so-called alien happened to be using numbers invented on earth. Or that these time travelers from outer space mark their calendars from the birth of Jesus the Earthman."

"Oh," Lizzie said, her confidence fading visibly. "But it made such sense. . . ."

"Stick to your pots," Remo said. He walked over to the line of heavy hanging draperies and yanked them down.

"What are you *doing*?" Lizzie shrieked. "Those are . . . Oh, my God."

They both stared in silence. For behind the draperies, beneath the panels of buttons and knobs and darkened lights, were four words they both read, again and again and again:

UNITED STATES OF AMERICA.

Chapter Ten

Captain's Log
8/21/2032

Our journey has begun—and perhaps ended—in calamity.

"Look at this," Lizzie said, drawing out a large book encased in plastic from a metal compartment. The beginning pages of the diary were filled with numbers and equations. The rest—hundreds of entries—were written in a hand that began with neat, controlled strokes and ended with a shaking, nearly illegible scrawl.

If we return, this document will serve as a record of our time here. If not, I will bury it upon its completion in the hope that some future generation might benefit from the experiences of myself and my crew on board the U.S. Cassandra.

Lizzie flipped through the log. The last hundred pages or so were blank. The author had either died before the diary was completed, or returned suddenly to his own time without it.

In case of the latter possibility—more a probability—now—I will put down briefly the facts of this mission, omitting all matter confidential to national security.

Our assignment was to test the time traveling device on board the craft. To do so without disturbing the course of history, we were to venture to a period long before the advent of human civilization, to 100,000 B.C. or further.

Although I cannot disclose the exact location of the experiment, it was to be in the southernmost region of the South American continent to eliminate any possibility of disrupting any form of human habitation which might have occurred at that time. We were to retrieve plant and animal specimens, and record our stay through constantly operating television cameras. We traveled with full space apparatus in tow, including protective clothing and oxygen equipment, as the atmospheric content at that time during the earth's evolution is uncertain.

The time module inside the fuselage of the Cassandra *operates on a principle of vibrating molecules triggered by shock-sensitive equipment. The system, I must submit, has no backup to prevent the mechanism from malfunctioning in the event of sudden movement, such as an emergency crash landing. To install such a secondary system would have required several more months of refinement, and everyone on earth knows that the Russians have for the past two years . . .*

The rest of the line was scratched out. The log took up again on the next line, the handwriting more stable.

That is inconsequential now. The worst has happened, and there is no call for complaint. All six of us volunteered for this mission, and all of us knew there were risks involved in accepting it.

More than a week ago, on 8/11/32, as we were passing over the area of the Central American Republic, one of the turbines blew. My engineer, Metters, is still working to determine and correct the problem. The malfunction resulted in a severe loss of balance for the Cassandra, *as she is made of Reardon metal, and lighter than aluminum. Although the Air Force has been utilizing craft constructed from Reardon for the past several years, no Reardon plane carrying the weight of our expedition has been used outside of tests.*

"The plane's made of something called Reardon metal," Lizzie said. "It's lighter than aluminum."

"And never rusts," Remo mused.

"It doesn't say, but I guess we can assume that."

We fell into a nosedive from which I could not pull out. When I felt certain that we would crash, I ordered the crew into the padded time module and set the computer to automatic, leaving it to either correct the malfunction or to land safely. Pilots, they say, are no longer necessary to aircraft except to oversee the running of electronic machinery.

The computer was no better a pilot than I was. Cassandra *crashed. Somehow, probably due to the resilience of the Reardon metal, the time module remained intact, although the craft was badly damaged and the video cameras utterly destroyed.*

The worst of it was that the time-traveling component, activated just after takeoff, was irreversible. Once the functioning of Cassandra *is placed onto computer-operated automatic pilot, all systems lock. When we emerged from the time module, we found that we had landed in the year the time system had reached at the moment of the crash—3114 B.C.*

We landed in the middle of a settlement of some kind, destroying several dwellings and killing at least twelve civilians. I recognize that I face court-martial for this offense, and accept any punishment the government of the United States chooses to impose on me.

The ruling body here, in this small city-state, has greeted us unexpectedly. Instead of hanging us, as they had every right to do, they have showered us with gifts and adoration, burying their dead without blame. They believe, I am certain, that we are deities from some far-off place.

The mission is already an unqualified disaster. Our cardinal rule—not to disturb the history of mankind—has been broken, due to unforseeable circumstances. Although my crew is taking pains to avoid contact with the people of this distant time, sleeping in our mylar tents in the immediate vicinity of the craft, eating from our rations, I cannot say how great an effect our arrival may cause here.

The most important decision is one I have put off making. Every day we see, from our limited vantage point, the struggle of these ancient people with common problems—sanitation, disease, building, irrigation—which even a child coming from our civilization could solve. It is difficult to watch the farmers plant their seeds on hillside slopes, knowing that their crops will be washed away with the rain. It is harder still to see mothers carrying babies covered with leeches in an attempt to cure malaria, when Chinchona bark—a known cure for the disease—is readily available in the local forest.

I do not know how long I can stand by, responsible as I am for the deaths of many of these people, without aiding them in some small way.

The crew is spending the whole of every day working on Cassandra, *attempting either to repair the time travel mechanism, or to get the craft into suitable condition to fly to a less inhabited location, where we could work on repairs without the constant fear of encroaching on this village. I do not know if either is possible.*

The entry was signed "Colonel Kurt Cooligan, U.S. Air Force."

"Guess there's not much doubt where 'Kukulcan' came from," Remo said.

Lizzie leafed through the pages absently. "Kurt Cooligan, the white god from the sky," she whispered. "Poor guy."

"From what we've seen here, it looks like he made his decision," Remo said. "Did he ever fix the time module?"

"I don't know yet," she said, skimming the pages rapidly. "Here's something about 'waves' . . . No, it's 'war.' His handwriting gets worse as he goes along."

"Must have been pretty hard on him."

"There's a lot about war. Some kind of war he got involved in here."

"The king told us that. Cooligan drove off some other tribe or something. Probably used guns—wait a second."

"The magic spears of fire," Lizzie remembered.

"Lasers. You saw them in the temple. Cooligan must have stashed them in here someplace." He set to searching the plane systematically as Lizzie read.

11/17/2032

There's no more point in hoping. Metters keeps working on the time module like a man possessed, but it's been three months. I don't think we'll ever get out of here alive.

"That's heartening," Lizzie said, feeling her heart sink.

"What?"

"A lot of help you are," she said. "Suppose you

did find the lasers. Do you think you can blast our way out of here?"

"Very funny. Do me a favor and mind your own business, okay?"

2/21/2033

I have given penicillin bread mold and Chinchona bark to the local healer, an old woman who delivers babies and makes herb teas for the dying. Communication was tough, but I think I got it across that one cures infections and the other malaria. She acted like they all do around me, as if I just blew in from Mars. I can't say I blame them, especially after the shoot-out we had with those crazy spearchuckers over the hill. Apparently the Olmec have been terrorizing this place for decades, raping and killing whoever got in their way. Unfortunately for all concerned, my plane and crew were the Olmec's target the last time. They haven't been back.

I don't like being a god, but they seem to have made me one. The king—an old timer who's as progressive as they come—just unveiled some ridiculous statue of "Kukulcan" (that's me) wearing my helmet. It took about thirty men to carry the thing over to the Cassandra.

I try not to interfere but, damn it, this is the best thing I've ever done. All the farms are planted in steps now, and the harvest these people get is unbelievable, what with the heavy rain and year-long summer. This mad king has even opened up trade with other villages down the road. Said road, incidentally, was designed by Major Bolam, botanist, copilot, and now civil engineer.

To hell with not interfering. We make a difference here, a big difference.

Sometimes I even manage to forget about Sandy and Michael.

"Sandy and Michael?" Lizzie said aloud.

"Huh?"

"Nothing. Did you find your guns?"

"Nope. What's Cooligan say?"

"He seems—happy."

"Terrific. Is he, by chance, happy because he discovered a way back to the twenty-first century?"

"No. Not yet, anyway."

"Some captain," Remo said in disgust, going over to the control panels.

"What are you doing?"

"I'm going to see if I can get this heap to work."

"Just like that? Don't you even need the flashlight?"

"No. My eyes adjust." He lifted off the lightweight metal panel and explored around the thousands of wires beneath it.

"You're serious, aren't you?" Lizzie asked, amazed.

"Would I lie to you?"

"Then why did you act like you needed light before?"

"So that you wouldn't ask me the kind of dumb questions you're asking me now," Remo said.

She dug back into the log.

7/2/2033

It's getting so hard to write. The headaches are happening almost every day now, and my vision is beginning to blur. It's no surprise. The doctor said this would happen. Glasses would help, for a while at least, but then glasses haven't been invented yet. Hah hah.

It's funny—now that my eyes are going, Sandy and Michael are clearer to me than ever. I guess the important things are what you see with your heart. That's pretty sloppy sentiment for a captain's log, but what the hell. Nobody's ever going to read this anyway.

Since I've been here these past fourteen months,

watching the crew's hopes turn into bad jokes, I've been giving a lot of thought to fate. The king—he's got a name a yard long, like everyone else in this place—says that our crash landing here was part of some prophecy. Like it was our destiny to blow out of the sky so we could build roads and invent mortar and teach these folks what zero is.

Bolam, our Renaissance man, is now supervising the construction of an observatory to read the stars with. I thought it was pretty crazy, but then, why not? What's a botanist got to do around a wrecked plane except go nuts? Metters, too. Sometimes I swear he's in love with the time module. He talks to it like a woman. He's already taken it apart and put it back together four times. He thinks he's getting close.

Let him play, too. We know our destiny, the king and I.

By the way, I've learned some of the language here. As the captain, I'm the official spokesman, but of course Bolam has picked it up, too. There's a guy who never should have enlisted. He's a born teacher, a real intellectual. Military life really held him back, I think.

I must admit I'm a lot freer myself than I used to be, but then I didn't want to be free before. If the truth be told, the U.S. Air Force was all that kept me from jumping off that bridge where Sandy and the baby crashed into the guardrail.

A blowout. A turbine malfunction. It's all the same, isn't it? You're going along, not doing too much of anything, and then fate steps in and gives you the finger. It's sure waving in my face now, 6,000 years away from home. But Sandy got worse than that.

I should never have let her drive that old clunker. Money was so tight then, but I should have made them take the bus. Or driven them myself. Then maybe she wouldn't have had the blowout and maybe she wouldn't have skidded into the guardrail, and maybe the car wouldn't have blown up and burned my baby son to death.

The military kept me together then. The rules, the routine, the other guys.

But I know I should have been in that car with them.

We've moved. After more than a year of sleeping in tents and foraging in the jungle like monkeys for food, I let the guys move into the rooms that the king set aside for us since we got here. It's in the royal palace, no less, with dancing girls and the works. Yesterday we played a game of baseball out on the grounds. We started out with teams of three, but all the local guys wanted to join in, and by the fourth inning there were more than twenty players on each team. I suppose baseball will turn into a national institution here, too. Then, afterward, the whole town got plastered on this brew made from fermented woodpeckers or something. Bolam, the botanist, was the worst of the lot. He has really changed. I didn't touch the stuff myself. Booze has the wrong effect on me. It makes me remember.

And now the headaches are starting, just like the good, discrete, private doctor said they would, and I made the mission, and the mission fizzled, and I'm going blind in a place where nobody can help me.

That's fate.

Sandy, I'm glad it's finally my turn.

Lizzie closed the book. "Remo, we've got to get out of here."

"Really? I hadn't thought about it," Remo said sarcastically. He looked up from the tangled mass of wires to see Lizzie's face glistening with tears. "Hey, what's the matter?"

She told him Cooligan's story. "He must have loved her so much," she said. "He was going blind, and all he could think about was his wife."

Oh, Dick. I've never even told you I loved you.

"Please try, Remo. I want to go home."

"I'm doing what I can," Remo said, winding two wires together. To his surprise, a hum began, low and erratic.

"You've done it," Lizzie gasped. "You fixed it!"

"Now cool it. I haven't done anything, except start a hum."

"That's a *motor*. That Metters guy must have fixed the module, after all. They all escaped!"

she cried jubilantly. "And we know where the switch is. We can make this thing take us back."

"How?" Remo asked.

"That's up to you. I'll get the others."

Chapter Eleven

"Quick, we're leaving," Lizzie shouted, interrupting Chiun's 450th stanza of an Ung poem about a bee lighting on a flower.

The court musicians playing behind him stopped abruptly. The king snorted out of deep slumber. In the corner of the king's throne room, where Po and Nata-Ah were playing dice, the spotted snakebones twirled in the air and landed in the silence with a dead thump.

"You have ruined my recital," Chiun said, clenching his jaws. "Now I will have to begin from the beginning."

"No, we have to leave now," Lizzie insisted. "Remo's got the mechanism working. Let's go."

Chiun stared at her acidly, deciding that the next time he came across a woman buried in stone he would leave her to rot. He made his apologies to the king through Po.

As Nata-Ah listened to the boy's explanation, tears filled her eyes. The boy turned to speak to her, but she scrambled to her feet and ran out of the room.

"Come on, come on. There's no time for this nonsense," Lizzie said, pushing the boy out.

In the temple, Lizzie gathered up all the priceless artifacts she could carry, plus the captain's log, and led the way into the pod.

"That is stealing," Chiun said coldly.

"This is archaeology," she retorted. "We need this as evidence that we've really been here. Besides, this temple was built for us, wasn't it?"

Remo looked up from the dials of the console. "No, it wasn't," he said softly. "It was built for some Irish pilot who played baseball and made medicine and then went blind. And he didn't take anything from here."

"We don't know that," she snapped. "For all we know, he took everything he could get his hands on. That old king's too old to know if anything's missing, anyway. Hurry up."

Remo shook his head and continued to work at the controls. The hum was getting louder.

As Po was walking reluctantly into the pod, the king and Nata-Ah appeared in the darkened doorway of the *Cassandra*. The boy started to move toward them, but Lizzie snatched him back.

"I'm sorry," Remo said. The king seemed to understand. He bowed to Chiun, then stood erect, his hand clasping the young girl's.

"If it does work, God only knows where we'll end up next. We might walk out of this thing and see a bunch of cavemen or futuristic mutants," Remo complained.

"Just set the dials right," Lizzie ordered.

Remo held his temper and set the dials. He pulled the broken switch. "I guess that's it," he said.

"Get in here," Lizzie shouted from inside the pod.

Ignoring her, Remo bowed to the king. The old man and his granddaughter both returned the bow. Then Remo climbed into the pod and closed the door to await the weird, syrupy sensations that would take him home.

"You interrupted my Ung poem for this?" Chiun said after several minutes.

"Nothing's happening," Lizzie said.

Remo stood up. "I told you all I started was a hum."

"You must have done something wrong!" Lizzie yelled, kicking open the door.

Outside, the king and Nata-Ah were still waiting. At the sight of the visitors, their faces lit up. The king began to sink to his knees, but Chiun held him up.

"No bowing," he said. "Those of our age bend to no man." Po translated, and the king led them back to the throne room.

"You have blessed me and my people by returning," the king said. "It is the time when we most need your services. You knew of our need and came back to us."

"What need?" Remo said.

"With Quintanodan returned to his tribe, the Olmec will be making ready to do battle against you."

"The Olmec are going to fight us?"

"But they will not win," the king assured him. "They cannot. For I have preserved something of Kukulcan's magic to aid you."

He led them behind a gold filigree screen, where a five-foot-tall jar of finest jade glowed. Lizzie's eyes popped at the sight. He bade Remo to remove the heavy lid of the jar and tip the vessel over. From its green mouth spilled six weapons made of greenish metal.

"The lasers," Remo said, picking one up. The light metal was strong as iron.

"The magic spears of fire," the king said, smiling. "For these ten years I have hidden them from all eyes, saving them for the return of our beloved Kukulcan. I had almost despaired of ever seeing the god again. But he has remembered my people. He has sent you in his place. These now, I know, belong to you." He started to bow, then straightened up with a smile to Chiun.

"Thank you, my friend," the old Oriental said. "But we have no need of these weapons now. When we return, my son will wish to take one to show his people. But if your enemies attack, we will fight them with our hands and our minds. Nothing else is necessary."

"Forgive me, wise one," the king said. "I should have known that Kukulcan would send other gods of different abilities, who fight in different ways." He smiled, and his eyelids drooped. "I am grateful, so grateful," he said, walking softly toward his gold and silver throne.

"You are weary," Chiun said. "Let us take you to your bed."

"No. I will remain here. There is much to be done in preparation for the attack of the Olmec. I will rest, but here, and just for a moment."

"As you wish," Chiun said. They left quietly.

From behind a panel of mirrors, a figure moved. The king was alone, and his heavy, even breathing filled the empty room. The man behind the mirror was dressed in a beggar's rags, but on his neck hung the precious topaz amulet of Quintanodan, high priest of the Olmec. He moved slowly, quietly as a cat, to the king's throne. Then, with practiced fingers, he encircled the old man's neck and squeezed. The king's eyes opened in silent terror.

"I have waited ten years to find the magic spears of fire," Quintanodan, the priest, whispered, staring directly into the king's face. "And now you have shown them to me. The Olmec will kill your people, destroy your gods, and level your kingdom to ashes. When you are gone, there will be nothing left of you but your rotting bones."

The king opened his mouth in a futile gesture. No sound came out. His face started to shake with spasms; his eyes bulged. He reached up with one trembling hand and clasped the topaz amulet, cold against his hot, numbing skin.

"Look in my eyes, old man, and despair," the priest whispered as he choked the life out of the dying king.

Chapter Twelve

"Read this," Lizzie said, handing Colonel Cooligan's log to Remo.

10/13/2033

Today we have an interesting project. Major Bolam, now the kingdom of Yaxbenhaltun's principal road builder, wants to construct a major trade route between this city and Chetumal Bay on the Gulf of Mexico, some 40 miles east. Bolam says the route will spur trade. I know what he's got in the back of his mind, though—a transatlantic crossing. I suppose nothing will stop Bolam in his quest for knowledge.

The main difficulty in surveying this route seems to be a local superstition about an area due east of here called, of all things, the Forbidden Fields. From all accounts, they lie between us and the caves of the Olmec.

The people here claim that the Olmec, who worship death, have poisoned the air of the fields, and Bolam's surveying team absolutely refuses to go. More than that, the king himself forbade my men to explore these so-called Forbidden Fields unless we use "magic" to protect us—meaning the oxygen equipment we were wearing when we first stepped out of the time module.

So I agreed. I figure there's no harm in wearing the equipment, at least until we're out of view of our hosts.

The Olmec themselves, I understand, keep far away from the fields, so I don't think we'll have any problems with them. I think it will just be a nice journey through some non-jungle countryside, and that will be a pleasant change for us all.

We'll build a road to the sea. Take that, Fate. Old Kukulcan, practically blind as a bat and no good for flying even if the Cassandra *suddenly decided to work, is not so bad, after all.*

I'm proud of all my men. They all know by now that we're never going to get out of here. Metters is even getting married to a local girl. When he does, I think I'll let him dismember Cassandra's *wiring so that he can invent electricity. The town could really use a generator for water. One of the other men has begun to draw up plans for a sewage system here.*

Malaria's already practically nonexistent now. That's my contribution. God, every time I see a little sick kid get well, I think of Michael, dying the way he did, and I wish I could have helped him. Maybe by helping these others I'm sort of helping him, too, in a roundabout way. I hope so.

We'll be together soon, Sandy and Michael and I. This disease I've got is supposed to progress geometrically. I guess the end will be pretty bad. Unfortunately, I don't know how to invent morphine for the pain. Well, nobody's perfect.

I can't say I'm glad about dying. It's funny, after I lost Sandy and the baby, dying was all I wanted. But this time I've spent here in Yaxbenhaltun has changed all that.

These people think the Olmec are the most evil thing they've got to worry about, but they're wrong. Disease is worse. So is ignorance. And poverty. And despair. My men and I have changed that for them, maybe forever. We've shot all to hell the cardinal rule about not changing the course of history, but one look at how these folks live now tells me it was all worth it.

Besides, maybe the king is right about this being our destiny. Who knows? Maybe one day the Mayans will be famous for being an advanced civilization. Maybe this is *the course of history, and we would have changed it by* not *coming. Very weird.*

This has been the greatest adventure any man could want. My crew knows that, and so do I.

I wouldn't have missed this for anything in the world.

The rest of the pages were blank.

"I wonder what happened to him," Remo mused.

"Simple. Metters got the module to work, and they all went home," Lizzie said confidently.

"Yeah," Remo said, trying to sound convincing. He knew that an experienced commanding officer who'd spent fifteen months trying to escape wouldn't leave without his weapons and his log. Cooligan had grown to love the people he'd lived among. He wouldn't have gone back to his time without saying good-bye. The colonel who had become a god had died, probably somewhere nearby.

From down the palace's long hallway came the terrified scream of a girl.

"Nata-Ah," Po said, jumping to his feet.

They found the girl running toward them in the hall. "My grandfather," she screamed, a topaz amulet dangling from her hand. "He is dead. The priest has murdered him." She ran past them to the palace's main entrance, shouting to the villagers to stop the evil priest.

But there was no priest. On the outskirts of the city, close to the fortified wall, walked a solitary figure dressed in rags and carrying a large sack over his back. No one paid attention to the beggar, or bothered to look inside the sack, where six laser weapons of green metal, the magic spears of fire of the gods themselves, rested.

"He's got to be here," the girl shouted. "Find him! Find the man who killed your king!"

The palace guards rushed into the square. Then, seemingly from out of nowhere, a horde of men, inconspicuous except for the black ash dot each wore on his forehead, rushed out of a thousand hiding places.

The guards fell first, their necks and chests spurting blood from the black knives that gleamed dully all around them. Then the screams of the villagers began as the Olmec blades sliced indiscriminately through the flesh of women and old men and those who had no defense.

Nata-Ah, her face a mask of unbelieving terror, rushed up to one of the killers as Po, limping, cursing himself for his slowness, came up shouting behind her. The killer swung wide, just missing the girl's throat. He forgot her immediately, lashing out with his long knife at others. Still fighting, he saw the limping boy out of the corner of his eye and kicked.

The blow struck Po square in the knees. His legs buckled with the pain, his vision dimming. As he struggled to retain consciousness, he saw a blur of blue, a garment on an old man who moved as swiftly as a wild bird, fly past him and imbedded two delicate fingers into the spine of the killer, stopping him forever.

"Take the right half of the square," Chiun commanded.

Remo obeyed, seeking out the black ash dots on the foreheads of the screaming, bleeding people in the square.

A knife flashed near him for a moment, and in another moment the knife was gone, along with the hand that held it.

A few yards away, a blade tore through the belly of a man fighting with a stick. The man screamed, watching his bowels spill onto the dirt in a gush of blood. Before the knife was withdrawn, Remo swatted the attacker's head with a flick of his hand, hearing the neck snap under his fingers. Another ash dot rushed at him. He clasped it in the center of his palm, crushing the skull behind it with one movement.

He let his body move automatically, instinctively. The days of frustration and inactivity were like an anger boiling inside him, and now he could permit it to come out. Too late to save the man with the stick, whose bloody entrails lay beside his corpse. But with speed, with thought, he and Chiun could fight for the others.

Lizzie, sobbing, dragged the two stunned children back into the entranceway. "Don't ever do that again," she shrieked into their faces. "You could have been killed, both of you. . . ."

Her tears dried instantly as she saw two Olmec, crouching and guarding their path with vicious slashes of their weapons, heading slowly toward the temple where the *Cassandra* lay.

"Oh, no. Not the pod," she whispered, feeling her throat constrict. She stood, horrified, releasing the hands of the children. "Remo!" she screamed. "They're going to destroy the plane!" But Remo was moving too fast to be seen.

"Wait here," she told Po. She ran as fast as she could toward the two Olmec warriors. "Stop it. Stop," she called, clawing at their sweating chests with her fingernails.

One of them clasped both her hands swiftly behind her back, his eyes flashing. The other smiled, with his mouth only, and nodded.

A full set of ribs cracked and imploded beneath the force of Remo's elbow. With a rattle of air, the warrior fell. Remo looked around. To his left, Chiun stood among the dead, his stance calm and ready. Around Remo lay the corpses, most of them with black dots on their foreheads. The remaining Olmec were in retreat, already disappearing into the thick jungle brush beyond the city walls.

In the palace entrance, Po held the weeping Nata-Ah in his thin arms.

"You two all right?" Remo asked.

Po nodded. "But Dr. Lizzie . . ."

Remo sighed. "What'd she do now?"

"They took her," the boy said. "She tried to guard the temple, but she was not strong enough to fight against the soldiers. They took her away with them."

Remo looked to the vast darkness of the jungle, feeling guilty about a certain relief he was experiencing. Lizzie had been nothing but trouble for them all since the beginning. Perhaps, now that she was gone, it would be possible to forget about her. . . .

"Leave her." It was Chiun. He seemed to read Remo's secret thoughts. "The woman is an unbearable harpy with no manners and no gratitude. You will risk your life for nothing."

Remo thought for a moment. "Yeah, you're right," he agreed, walking away from the palace.

"Where are you going?"

"To get her," Remo said resignedly.

"Why?" Chiun's voice was stern. "You are needed here. Who cares about her?"

Remo turned around. "Nobody," he said. "That's why I'm going."

Chapter Thirteen

The trail leading from the city was easy to follow. The rush of departing Olmec had worn the jungle undergrowth to a well-traveled footpath. It wound past Bocatan to a marsh, where the muddy, ankle-deep water still churned with the recent agitation of dozens of feet.

Remo followed the marsh, swarming with mosquitoes and jungle rats, surrounded by giant ferns grown to the proportions of trees, until the water cleared. Where had they gone?

The sky was fading to early twilight, that time of day when nothing is seen perfectly, when the sky is half light and half shadow, blue alternating with gray, the color of thunderclouds. He narrowed his vision to take in distance. Past the marsh was a row passing through a flat field, grassy as the savannahs of western Africa, where no trees grew. The row looked like flattened grass created by footsteps. But it was too narrow for all the Olmec who had left the square at

Yaxbenhaltun. Had they walked in single file? Why?

There was no time to think it over. He stepped out of the marsh to follow the path made through the recently trampled grass.

Two sets of footprints. He was sure of it. Fading light or not, no more than two people had made the path Remo was following. It didn't make sense, but he tracked it doggedly, the bottoms of his trousers growing wet from contact with the high, damp grass. The field stretched for miles, widening after the marsh so that it seemed to go on forever in all directions, green, green grass dotted occasionally by white flowers. As he went on, the flowers grew more numerous, bringing with them the sweet, drugged air Remo remembered. By the time he had followed the footprints for a mile, the flowers blanketed the ground.

Remo's eyelids drooped. He would have to slow his breathing to keep from falling asleep again. Slowly he pumped the air out from his lungs and breathed shallowly, ever more slowly, feeling his heartbeat drop from fifty beats a minute to forty to thirty to ten. His mind cleared somewhat. Still, the delicious fragrance of the field, looking as if it were covered with snow, seeped into his lungs and his mind and teased him with sensual promise.

The Forbidden Fields . . . Kukulcan's last mission, Remo remembered. Something about building a road. Going to the sea, and going blind. Cooligan of the Forbidden Fields. *The flowers killed him, can't you see?*

Remo gasped. The swift intake of air sent his senses reeling. He calmed himself, making the white-covered fields stop whirling around him. But when he did, the sight in front of him was still there. Not more than twenty feet away, the trail ended. It ended with the prostrate bodies of two men whose uniforms identified them as members of the palace guard.

He turned them over. Their faces were blue, their bodies already beginning to stiffen and cool. A trap. The two men must have been taken prisoner and set off to walk through the Forbidden Fields until they dropped, while the Olmec took Lizzie on some other route.

He looked around. The fields stretched to every horizon, broken only by the rounded tops of huge rocks. He stilled himself, forcing his breathing to come even more slowly, consciously enlarging his senses to take it every sight, every sound.

There was water. Somewhere. The river, Remo said to himself. If he could find water—a stream, a trickle—he could follow it to the river and get his bearings from there.

The sweet fragrance lingered. The air was thick with it; there was no way to blot out the cloying, sleep-filled scent of the white flowers that beckoned him to rest among their soft petals.

Water. Follow the sound of the water.

He dragged on. Night seemed to fall palpably

as he walked, then crawled, following a sound he was no longer sure he heard. The wind in the flowers, sending up its thick, forgetful smoke, drowned out every other sensation with its haunting music.

Remember the water.

And there was water. A swirling river of it, crashing and dancing between a thousand white stones. He shook his head to see if the water were no more than a clouded vision. But it remained, he could smell it, he could feel its cool mist enveloping him. He stood upright, blinking against the lightheadedness that willed him back to the ground. He walked downstream, plodding like a man dying of thirst in the desert, until he stood beside the crest of a small, low fall where the water rushed white and bubbling. And on the crest was a woman, shrouded in mist, naked except for the thick ring of white flowers around her neck, her hair golden. She turned slowly toward him, holding out her arms.

It was Elizabeth Drake.

As if he were in a dream, Remo went to her, stepping through the shallow water at the top of the fall. She smiled. There was no hardness about her now, no cranky modernity. She was Woman, eternal and ageless, soft in her mystery, calling him silently to her.

Without thought, he embraced her. In that moment, their lips touching, his body aching for her, he took in the scent of the flowers, luxurious, devastating, smelling of sin and ecstasy, and gave in to it.

The sky darkened. The earth fell away. He was complete.

He awoke next to her. His clothes were still wet from the mist of the waterfall, and they clung coldly to his skin. Beside him, on the stone floor where they lay, he could feel Lizzie shivering in her sleep.

His head was pounding. He tried to sit up, but the movement was too difficult for him. Part of him, a great part, wanted just to go back to sleep, despite the cold and the wet and the uncertainty. But the other part of him, that part which was Remo, had to stay awake. He had to force himself out of the feeling of drunkenness and uncaring that seemed to hang over him like a sheet.

He willed his eyes wide open. The first items they focused on were the barrels of the six laser weapons, surrounding the two prisoners in a circle. Their guards, six tall, rangy men with tattoos on their bellies and black ash dots decorating their foreheads, kept at a distance from them both.

No sweat, Remo thought thickly. One turn, a spiral air attack, and . . .

He couldn't move. Thick ropes cut into his wrists and ankles. Ropes? How had he permitted himself to be tied like a pig going to slaughter?

And then he smelled them. Fresh, enchanting, the scent of the white flowers assaulted his newly awakened senses from the heavy garland he wore around his neck. Lizzie wore one, too, and their perfume weakened and sickened him.

They were in a cave. Behind the fragrance of the flowers, Remo could pick out the dank odor of damp earth. The walls, painted with pictures of grotesquely endowed human figures engaged in sexual activity, were lit by oily torches that sent up strings of black smoke.

The guards seemed to be part of the tableau. Motionless, their fingers poised on the triggers of the lasers, they watched the prisoners. The flesh on their faces sagged with the effort of fighting off sleep.

They're getting drugged too, Remo thought. The white flowers around their necks were affecting the guards. It would be so easy. So easy . . . But Remo did not struggle against the ropes. There was still time for fighting, and he had no advantage now. He would wait.

He looked over at Lizzie. She lay beside him, naked, unconscious, her clothes in a bundle at one of the guards' feet.

She was neither harpy nor goddess now, just another poor sucker who had been pushed senselessly into a nightmare that might end her life. As Colonel Cooligan had so eloquently written, fate had given them all the finger.

Lizzie was a strange woman. She was as selfish and abrasive as they came, a bra burner of the first water. Yet she had cried over Cooligan's diary. And when the thick of the battle with the Olmec was around her, she had tried to save the time module.

And succeeded. The Olmec had taken prisoners, but they hadn't destroyed the *Cassandra.* Good for you, Lizzie.

He closed his eyes. Sleep would feel good. A long, pleasant sleep to let go in, a sleep of endless dreams . . .

The harsh voice of a man sounded above him, jarring and loud. It struck his senses awake like a physical blow. By his head, the priest Quintanodan stood, leering.

The priest had changed much. The sharp aristocratic features of his face were painted with rough strokes of white and black, to match the ash dot on his forehead. His hair was matted and awry, falling in ropy strands on his bare, oiled shoulders. He was naked except for a strip of jaguar skin around his loins, and two ringlets of brown feathers on his ankles.

Overhead Remo could feel the vibrations of a hundred feet. The Olmec, he figured, preparing to attack Yaxbenhaltun in force. They had the lasers now. It would not take long to destroy the city.

A chuckle began deep in Quintanodan's throat and grew until it resonated through the dank cave. Then, spitting out a command to the guards, he was gone.

Snapping to attention, the guards kicked Remo and Lizzie to their feet. Lizzie stumbled, moaning.

"It's so cold," she said.

"They're moving us."

"For what, a firing squad?" she said, her unclothed body beautiful in the torchlight.

It wasn't the end, Remo knew. If worse came to worst, he would attack the guards and then fight his way through the other soldiers. But the powerful scent of the white flowers around his neck had weakened him—not enough to stop him, but perhaps enough to throw off his timing to the point where a stray beam from one of the lasers could get to Lizzie and fry her. He would have to get himself free of the flowers before he could work effectively.

But Lizzie didn't know that. To her, the guards were taking them on their last journey. And she was still holding up, bad jokes and all. She was tough, Remo had to give her that.

One of the guards picked up Lizzie's clothes and thrust them roughly at her. She clung to them with her bound hands. "What's that noise up there?" she asked.

"Soldiers, I think. Now that the Olmec have the lasers, they're probably going to attack everything in sight."

"Oh, wonderful," Lizzie said. "There goes history. The twentieth century will never have heard of the great Mayan civilization."

"Maybe it'll be the great Olmec civilization."

Lizzie sniffed. "These animals? They couldn't care less about astronomy or mathematics or engineering. This land will be like the aftermath of the Roman Empire—how it became after it was conquered by savage hill tribes. All of the learning, all of the Maya's work will be lost. Everything Cooligan did will be gone forever."

The guards stopped them in front of a rounded entranceway and shoved them inside, sealing the way behind them with a rock.

"Even cavemen had prisons, I guess," Remo said. Inside the entranceway stood a huge stone demon with eyes of jade.

"Puch," Lizzie said. "God of the dead. How appropriate."

"Don't knock it," Remo said, bending low at the waist. "Getting locked up here is the luckiest thing that's happened to us yet."

"What are you talking about?"

The garland of flowers fell from around his neck to the floor. Raising his bound hands, he snatched Lizzie's necklace and tore it off as well, kicking both strings of the white flowers into a corner. "I was hoping they'd leave us alone," Remo said. "Give me a couple of minutes."

He retreated into the shadows of the stone vault. Away from the weakening fragrance of the flowers, he could at last breathe deeply. The musty air of the vault filled him with new strength, charging his muscles like electricity.

A small line of light lay on the floor. He looked up. Moonlight. It was coming from a crack in the overhead rock. Good, Remo thought. I can use that.

A few feet away lay, inexplicably, a bed of coal smoothed into a square. "Whatever that is, I can use it, too," he muttered.

The ropes strained against his wrists. Breathing rhythmically, concentrating, Remo clenched his hands into fists, rotating them slowly. As he did, the fibers of the ropes snapped, one by one, unraveling in front of his eyes.

At the same time he tensed the muscles in his calves so that the ropes over his ankles frayed and broke. With a pop, both ropes fell away from him at precisely the same moment, landing on the stone floor like discarded snakeskins.

"How'd you do that?" Lizzie asked incredulously.

"Never mind." Effortlessly he snapped the ropes around Lizzie's wrists and legs. "Get dressed."

His strength was back. Escaping would be no problem, not with a half-inch-wide crack in the rock. He explored the fissure with his fingers.

He could break through the rock easily, but it would make a lot of noise, alerting the Olmec warriors. He didn't want a fight now, with Lizzie around. Also, the Olmec didn't fight to the last man. Even the small group of warriors sent for the surprise attack on Yaxbenhaltun had retreated when they were getting beaten. As soon as Remo started fighting, he knew, the priest in charge of the Olmec would send as many of his men off to Yaxbenhaltun, willing to sacrifice a few soldiers in order to keep Remo away from the people who needed him to defend them.

No, the escape would have to be silent. Lizzie would have to be taken back to safety. Then Remo would return with Chiun to dispose of the Olmec—all of them—in their own camp.

He ran his fingernails over the crack in the rock, familiarizing his hands with the natural curve of the break. The rock would have to be cleaved according to its fault in order to break it silently.

Feeling the weakened area of stone, he set up a vibration in his hands. Slowly, with a sound that only Remo could hear, a sound like metal on a chalkboard, his fingernails cut through the rock, forming a circle. When the work was finished, he raised the stone disc above him like a manhole cover and moved it.

A stream of moonlight flooded into the cave. Lizzie stood, awestruck, watching him.

"Come on," Remo whispered, motioning her toward the exit he had carved out of the rock. "We don't have much—"

The words froze in his mouth. Something was behind Lizzie, illuminated now by the moonlight, something low and long and immobile and ghastly.

He spoke softly. "Liz, I'm going to ask you a favor, okay?"

She nodded.

"Just listen to what I tell you. You can't make any noise now, not for any reason. The Olmec aren't far away. They can't see us, but they'll come running if you scream. So whatever happens, keep your mouth shut. Got it?"

She started to tremble. "There's something behind me, isn't there?" she whispered.

"Nothing that'll hurt you."

She turned slowly. Her eyes widened for a

moment, then closed tightly, trying to block out the sight. Her hands flew, shaking, to her face.

On a low stone slab lay the body of a man dressed in an astronaut's protective clothing. On his shoulder was an American flag. His helmet was missing. All that remained of his face was an exposed skull. In the center of his forehead was a sharp, ragged hole.

Remo climbed down to look at the body. As Lizzie watched, he unzipped the plastic closure on the front of the man's protective coveralls. Inside, on the shirt covering the skeleton, was a plastic tag with "Col. K. Cooligan" inscribed on it.

They had found the final resting place of the white god Kukulcan.

Chapter Fourteen

Lizzie stood rooted in her tracks, trembling, her hands covering her face. "Get going," Remo said, grabbing her by both shoulders and propelling her toward the exit he had made. She climbed out of the hole and scrambled blindly toward the dark forest behind the Olmec's cave dwellings.

"Where are you going?" Remo whispered.

"The trees," she said, bewildered. "That's how we came, isn't it?"

"The trees?" Of course. The Olmec had taken Lizzie through the forest, bypassing the Forbidden Fields, with their strange evil blossoms. They could make it through the jungle tangle, following the sound of the river, as far as the marsh. Then they would walk toward Bocatan, the volcano, to Yaxbenhaltun.

"Good girl," Remo said. "I mean—"

"That's okay," Lizzie answered, clasping his hand as they entered the black jungle. "Names don't matter. You came back to get me. That makes two times that you've saved my life. Thanks, Remo. You deserve an apology from me."

He laughed. "I never thought I'd hear that."

"It's the truth, and the truth ought to be spoken. While there's still time."

"You're thinking about that Diehl guy back home, aren't you?"

She looked up, startled. "No. No, really—"

"Don't start lying to me now," Remo said, smiling. "I'm just beginning to get used to you the way you are." A macaw shrieked overhead. "What happened at the waterfall between us was great, but I wasn't who you were thinking about," he said.

She looked into his eyes for a long moment. "You still surprise me," she said.

"How'd you wind up on top of a waterfall, anyway?"

She thought. "I came to somewhere in this forest," she said. "One of the Olmec showed up with the garland of flowers and put it around my neck. From then on, I don't remember much, except standing on top of the waterfall. I was trying to keep from falling asleep. I thought that's what the Olmec had planned for me—to fall asleep and then go crashing on the rocks at the foot of the fall. They'd taken my clothes. . . . And then you were there." She stopped and pulled him to her. "I'd never been so happy to see anyone in my life."

He pulled away from her. "Not as happy as you'll be to see Dick Diehl again."

She sighed. "It's too late for that," she said, breathing in the clean, damp air of the rain forest with its thousand birds calling in the night. "I thought that if I could impress him with my brilliance, he'd want me. Now I only wish I had told him that I cared about him." She chuckled. "Not that Dick would have noticed, anyway. Anything that's not made of stone and over a thousand years old has no interest for him."

"Don't wait that long," Remo said.

"Now, don't *you* start lying to *me*," she said gently. "We're not going anywhere. Even if you get rid of the Olmec, we'll still be here. Cooligan couldn't get out, and his crew knew the machinery of that time module better than we do." She squeezed his hand. "So no false hopes between us, okay?"

"Okay," Remo said.

As they came closer to the volcano, Remo spotted a dot of red glowing at its peak. "Are you seeing what I'm seeing?"

"Lava. It's swollen, too."

"What, the volcano?"

"Look at the shape of it." She pointed to the black outline of Bocatan in the moonlit sky.

"It almost looks as if the volcano's pregnant."

"So she is," Lizzie said. "They get that way when they're about to erupt."

"Erupt when?"

"Can't say. Tonight, a month—it varies."

"Hey, that thing can't erupt," Remo protested.

"It's been dead for years. At least not since the beginning of the town. As close as Yaxbenhaltun is, it'd get wiped out if the volcano blew."

"Sometimes volcanoes wait hundreds of years between eruptions. Bocatan may have last gone off before Yaxbenhaltun was built. Cooligan got things moving pretty fast, remember?"

Remo stood staring at the red glow for a moment. "I've got an idea," he said.

They climbed to the top of the volcano, feeling the mountain gurgle and swim beneath their feet.

"Look, if I've got a choice, I'd rather be zapped by a laser beam than drowned in lava," Lizzie said.

"Nothing's going to happen. Especially now." With a large rock he picked and pulled at the lip of the volcano until the eastern portion of it was two feet lower than the rest, exactly on a level with the bubbling lava inside.

"What's that for?" Lizzie asked.

"You'll see."

Back in Yaxbenhaltun, he announced the plan. "Po, I want you to get every available man to get to the volcano as fast as possible and collect all the stones they can, enough to make the lava overflow."

"You will start an eruption?" Po asked.

"Nah. You can't make a volcano blow with a few stones. I just want it to spill over a little onto the Olmec's side. I've fixed it so that it will."

He turned to Chiun. "Meanwhile, you and I will go back to the Olmec camp and take back the lasers. By the time the volcano begins to overflow, we'll have the guns, and the Olmec'll be scared out of their pants. That'll be where you come in with one of your Master of Sinanju speeches."

"I do not speak their language," Chiun said curtly.

"That doesn't matter. You point to the overflowing volcano, say 'Kukulcan' a couple of times, and they'll keep away from this place for the rest of their lives. And no lives lost, no interruption of history. It's worth a shot, isn't it?"

Chiun's eyes narrowed. "The boy is right. What if the volcano erupts?"

"I tell you, it's not going to erupt."

"Oh, yes it will," Lizzie said. "It shows all the signs."

"Well, it's not going to erupt tonight. Let's go through with this plan and worry about the volcano later."

Reluctantly they agreed. Po went out to gather all the able-bodied men of the city. Chiun and Remo stole out through the jungle toward the caves of the Olmec.

They stayed close to the river, keeping an eye on the glowing rim of Bocatan. The sky changed from black to blue to slate gray; the crisp crescent moon grew fuzzy and small overhead. By the first red streaks of dawn, the silhouettes of a hundred Mayan warriors stood around the volcano's red mouth.

"Oh, balls," Remo said. "They're not supposed to be there yet."

"It is a beautiful sight," Chiun said. "Worthy even of a stanza of Ung poetry."

"Poetic, maybe. But too soon. The idea was for us to get to the Olmec caves *before* the Mayans showed themselves."

"No plan works perfectly," Chiun said philosophically.

The Mayans remained on the mountaintop, bending and straightening as they placed their stones carefully inside the brimming volcano.

"Too early, too early," Remo muttered, skittering as quickly as he could through the slimy mud of the river's edge. At Bocatan, a thin stream of red lava poured down the side of the sacred fire mountain.

"Will you look at that," Remo said, disgusted. "The whole plan's ruined."

"It was a stupid plan," Chiun agreed. "But what can one expect of a white man?"

"Now the whole effect will be . . ." He stopped. "Hey, there hasn't *been* any effect. No yelling, no stampede from the caves, nothing."

"Perhaps the Olmec are not the dunderheads you assumed them to be," Chiun said.

"What does that mean?"

The old Oriental shrugged. "Only that your escape may have been detected. Did you think of that?"

"Well—"

"Of course not. At your age, one considers only action, never reaction. You never gave any thought to what the Olmec would do if they discovered your absence, did you?"

"What would you do if you were an Olmec?" Remo asked.

"Just what they have done. I would wait."

"Where?"

"Here."

The old man shoved Remo to the ground. In that moment, the sky lit up with six shafts of white lightning, causing the dark jungle brush to burst into flames and the water of the river to shimmer like silver. On the peak of Bocatan, no less than twenty men fell, their silhouetted postures those of men dying in agony.

"Why didn't you tell me?"

"It was only now that I became certain of it. Find the men with the guns. They must go first."

They fought their way through the onrush of Olmec warriors, seeking the laser bearers in the rear flanks.

Accustomed to jungle fighting, the Olmec splintered and fled, scattering in all directions so that they could not be taken in a single assault. Remo worked his way through the ranks of warriors, but not a single laser blast was seen again.

"Where'd they go?" Remo said as he launched two Olmec into a double air spin to collide with the soldiers behind them.

Then they came again, the dazzling spears of light that bored holes into the sides of Bocatan. The origin of the beams was high overhead, and considerably closer to the Mayan camp than Remo and Chiun were.

"They're in the trees," Remo said despairingly.

"We've been fighting down here, and those guys with the lasers have been moving ahead through the frigging trees." Without waiting for Chiun to speak, he climbed up a tall jujube tree and scrambled over its branches to the next.

They were dangerously close to Bocatan. The Mayans, with no leader, were no match for the warring Olmec with their weapons from the twenty-first century. There was only one way to stop them from swarming over the volcano into the city of Yaxbenhaltun: Remo would have to create a distraction that would give Chiun enough time to work his way through the foot soldiers and then take out the laser bearers.

When he reached the marsh, past the Forbidden Fields, he ran at double time toward the volcano. Earlier, when he had climbed the eastern slope of Bocatan with Lizzie, they had made their way up a narrow pass. If he could collect the Olmec there, Chiun would have an easier time of getting rid of them.

He approached the pass minutes before the six Olmec.

"Hey, you fruits, hubba hubba," he shouted to the oncoming warriors. A laser shimmered in the air toward him. It struck the exact location where he stood, but in the split second it took the beam to travel, Remo was gone. The shaft dug a deep crater into the side of the volcano.

"That's good, fellas. Just what I wanted." He stuck his thumbs into his ears and blurted a rasberry at the confused soldiers. "Come on, creeps, it's target practice."

Another laser lit up the sky, striking the hillside. And another.

"Chiun, get a move on, will you?"

"Watch your tone of voice," Chiun said indignantly from the shadows. He leaped high in the air, taking off the top of a man's head in his descent.

"Good work, Little Father."

"Mind your own affairs."

Remo was ready. One of the warriors, aiming his weapon directly at him, stood in firing position, open from every angle.

"The problem with guns," Remo said as the man's finger moved back imperceptibly on the trigger, "is that your body is wasted." He spun out of the way of the fiery charge. The soldier tried to get a bead on him again, but he was gone.

"The only part of your body you use with a gun is your finger, see," Remo said from behind him. The warrior spun around. No one was there.

"The rest of you is completely vulnerable." The soldier turned again, firing without looking. The beam tore into the side of the mountain.

"See what I mean?" Remo said, delivering a kick to the man's kidneys that turned them to brown jelly. The corpse's fingers twitched spasmodically on the sensitive trigger. A burst of fire sliced into Bocatan's worn and pitted slope. Remo reached the weapon and crushed it to gravel in his hands.

"Okay, who's next?" he shouted. Chiun was in

the process of splintering someone's neck into a thousand pieces with a rapid drum of his fingers. The man's weapon soared upward. The other laser bearers were fleeing back toward the caves. "Oh, no you don't," Remo said. "You're not getting another chance, Bonzo." He took off after the man, caught him, and smashed his weapon to shards in front of his face.

The man's mouth dropped open.

Remo said, "You were willing to fight me when you had the laser. Now I insist we go on."

But the man only sputtered, his eyes staring straight ahead of him. He raised a violently shaking finger and pointed behind Remo's back.

"Come on," Remo said in disgust. "That's old. I look behind me and you get a chance to break my nose. Well, it doesn't work that way, chum." He tossed the man to the ground, looked behind him, and within a half a second picked the man up again. "See? Oh, God."

Bocatan was cracking open before his eyes.

The probes made by the lasers had torn her surface to shreds. Now the swollen volcano glowed red from its gurgling mouth to its base, streaked with deep fissures where pulsating red liquid oozed out.

"Remo!" Chiun shouted from the far rim of the volcano's peak. "Leave the warriors."

"Gotcha," Remo said, suddenly remembering the Olmec soldier supported in his hands. Almost absently he tapped the man's solar plexus. The man slumped to the ground.

And the fire mountain exploded.

Its entire eastern side blew in a stream of lava shooting from its base. The red mouth of the volcano darkened and receded as the lava spewed out of its collapsing side.

The heat and force of the molten rock blew Remo aside like a weightless feather as it tumbled onto the valley, swallowing rocks whole and burning a blinding path past the marsh and into the Forbidden Fields, where the burning miles of white flowers gave off a stench of sweet decay.

Above the din of the collapsing volcano could be heard the wails of the Olmec trapped in the inexorable flow of molten death, their screams sounding like the chattering of small birds, insignificant in the roaring eruption.

A man, his face burned horribly, ran toward Remo carrying a long-bladed knife in his hands. The entire top half of his body was blackened. On his shoulders were huge bubbling blisters, sprouting from deep within the muscle tissue. Remo could tell the man wouldn't last for ten minutes.

"Don't put yourself through the trouble," Remo said, taking the knife. The man covered his face with his charred hands.

"I'll help you to die," Remo said quietly, placing his arms around the man's body so that he would feel as little pain as possible. Then, with two fingers, Remo prepared to touch a cluster of nerves at the base of the man's throat that would put him to sleep painlessly and forever.

As if he could read Remo's thoughts, his eyes widened. In a burst of strength he pushed himself away.

"You're him, aren't you?" Remo said. "Quintanodan."

At the sound of his name, the priest painfully pulled himself erect. Even through his burned flesh and obvious agony, Quintanodan's expression retained all of its arrogance and cruel authority. He pointed to the rim of Bocatan, where the Mayans watched the inferno below in awed silence.

"You want me to take you there, huh?" Remo said, gesturing.

The priest nodded curtly.

"Why should I? You didn't exactly treat me like your long lost brother. Not to mention your hospitality toward Cooligan."

Again, the dying priest seemed to know what Remo was thinking. He blinked rapidly, striving to keep his eyes in focus. Clearly the man was losing consciousness. Then, with great effort, he bowed to Remo.

"Oh, cut it out," Remo said, picking the man up deftly. The movement, gentle as Remo tried to make it, must have been excrutiating. Still, the priest made no sound. "I guess you're not going to hurt anyone now."

Good guys and bad guys, killers and saints . . . In their final moment, all men knew terror. It was Quintanodan's moment now, and Remo respected it.

He did not despise the man for being a killer. Remo was one himself, after all, and although he had known since the death of the old king that Quintanodan would have to die, Remo was hard pressed to feel any hatred for him now. He had looked into the eyes of too many dying men to hate an enemy in torment. All life was sacred in the moment it was extinguished.

And so he carried the priest to the top of Bocatan, steaming above the destruction in the valley.

Quintanodan, lying on his back, beckoned to the boy Po to come near him while he spoke. The boy translated the man's anguished words.

"It is written that the voice of the gods will come to rule the Maya and defeat their enemies," he said. "The prophecy has come to pass. My people are dispersed, my tribe decimated. But you will not rule forever, because the Olmec understand what you do not: that the past and the future are one. That which flourishes must decay. That which lives now must return to its ashes. My people are clever. Many have died this day, but others have fled to wait, to fight again. Two of the gods' weapons remain. They are well hidden now, but one day they will be found.

"I have come to tell you this. We will fight you one day, and on that day we will defeat you. Until then, we will wait in secret. The name of the Olmec will be no more. But when our time comes, your empire will crumble to dust at our hands. For all the ages of man, no one will know why the great Mayan civilization vanished, but you will know, and your children, and your children's children, for I speak from the Sight, and the Sight does not lie. Ages hence, the Olmec will conquer you, you will be as dust in the wind of the sea."

He stood up painfully, rivulets of sweat running down his disfigured features. He faced the gaping mouth of the volcano and repeated an ancient prayer:

"All moons, all years, all days, all winds, take their course and pass away."

He held his blackened arms over his head. Then, his face composed, his mouth set, he dived into the distended mouth of the volcano, making no sound as he died.

The Mayans standing atop Bocatan turned to Remo and Chiun and knelt. Dawn flooded the sky with red, looking through the smoke and steam like a vision from hell.

The moment lingered forever, it seemed. Each man tried to take a measure of the events of the past twenty-four hours, and could only remember it as a time of great moment, its details already fading into the realm of legend. Only Chiun remained entirely in the present, lowering himself to the ground, listening.

"What are you doing, Little Father?" Remo said, noticing the strange posture of the old Oriental.

"Take them away from here," Chiun said.

"Why?"

The old man spoke softly. "Earthquake."

The boy was the first to respond. "Nata-Ah," he cried, limping as fast as he could toward the village, where the women and children of Yax-benhaltun slept.

Chapter Fifteen

The limestone columns of the palace were already crashing by the time the boy reached it. Remo was inside, pulling the women and the household staff to safety, while Chiun and Lizzie worked with the Mayan warriors to wake the rest of the village.

"Where is Nata-Ah?" Po asked.

"I can't find her. Maybe she's already out."

"She is not. She must be here!" the boy bellowed.

"Look, I've got enough on my hands," Remo said, pulling a bevy of shrieking dancing girls through the falling rock. "The building's full, and it's going to go fast, so get out of the way."

"I will help," the boy said, rushing into the palace. Two old women, balancing a load of clay dishes between them, tottered from the kitchen, blocking the hall where others screamed behind them. The boy knocked the dishes out of their hands and pushed them forward, making room for the stampede.

"Nata-Ah!" he called, forcing his way against the crowd. He scanned the panicking faces that swept past him, but the beautiful young girl was not among them.

Po made his way into the interior of the palace, where the ornate painted ceilings dipped and swayed rhythmically to the deep rumbles of the earthquake. The roof would cave in within minutes with him inside, unless he got out quickly. But Nata-Ah. What if she was still somewhere in the palace?

He walked under the buckling ceiling of the reception hall and into the labyrinth of the palace's great rooms.

"Nata-Ah!" he shouted, but his voice was drowned out in the splintering crash of stone on ground outside.

She was not in the room where she normally slept. The other rooms were also empty, their doors hanging open. Only the king's throne room was sealed.

He burst in. The girl was inside, sitting straight and tall upon her grandfather's magnificent throne.

"Nata-Ah, you must come. There is danger," Po said in the Old Tongue.

"This is the end of the world," the girl said softly. "I am the world's ruler now. I will remain here."

"Oh, Nata-Ah," Po pleaded. "There is so much I have to tell you. This isn't the end. It's just the beginning. Me, I come from the end, not you. Your people will make a mark on history that will never be forgotten, never."

"You know this?"

"Yes, I know."

"You are the voice of the gods, just as my grandfather said. You are like Quintanodan. You have the Sight."

"Nata-Ah, your grandfather was only setting a trap for Quintanodan when he called me that. And I don't have the Sight. It's just that I come from—"

"You came with the gods," she said. "And you will leave with them. And I will remain here, for I do not wish to live without you." Her eyes shone with tears.

He was stunned. Long moments passed. Down the hall, the ceiling burst and a ton of rock poured into the smashed palace with a sound like thunder. The door to the throne room flew open and creaked mightily, twisting out of shape as an ocean of debris showered behind it.

Po touched her face. "Then I will stay here with you," he said. "For you are all I need in this life. I have followed you forever, and now that I have found you, I will stay to my last breath at your side."

Suddenly, through the wreckage, a man appeared.

"What the hell are you two doing here?" Remo yelled angrily, grabbing each child in one hand and vaulting to the window. "Hang on." He tumbled outside, leaping over the piles of fallen cement to safety.

"You've got rocks in your heads, both of you," he shouted over his shoulder as he ran toward the square. "When this is over with, I'm going to spank the daylights—"

"Remo," Lizzie shouted excitedly.

"I don't have time," Remo said.

"But it's an *earthquake*. That's what brought us here in the first place. 'The vibration of molecules,' that's what Cooligan said made the time module work."

Remo pulled a screaming man from beneath a slab of rock. "If an earthquake's all it took, then why didn't Cooligan get out during one?"

"Because while Cooligan was here, *there wasn't an earthquake*. Not one is mentioned in the log. He never had the chance, but we do. Come *on*," she said, pulling at his arm. "Get the others. It has to be now."

Remo straightened up. He swept his arm over the scene around him. The entire city was a wreckage. White plaster and dust covered the faces of the dead on the street. Hundreds of small fires burned everywhere. "We can't go, Lizzie. People's lives are still in danger. In a few minutes, when the earthquake's subsided, maybe—"

"We can't wait for it to subside! This is the only chance we're going to get, and you know it. If the pod hasn't already been damaged, that is. A few more minutes, and the temple holding the *Cassandra* might be destroyed."

"We've just got to wait," Remo said stubbornly.

"I don't have to do any such thing," she screamed. "This is my last shot to get out of here, and by God, I'm going to take it!"

"All by yourself? What if the mechanism won't work again?"

"That's your problem," Lizzie said.

Remo shook his head. "Guess I was wrong about you, old girl. Still looking out for number one, aren't you?"

"Can you blame me?"

Remo looked closely at her, and then at the ruin of the city. "No, I can't. I'm the same way myself. No strings, no responsibilities. He travels fastest who travels alone."

Lizzie regarded him suspiciously. "Then why aren't you coming?" she asked.

Remo looked out over the far horizon, shimmering in the wake of the city's flames. "Because I'm tired of hating myself," he said.

Her eyes hardened. "If you think that this is going to make me—"

"I wasn't talking about you. I was talking about me."

Struggling to keep her face impassive, she stood watching him for a moment. Then she turned and strode away.

"Well, that's that for the moment," Remo said.

Most of the rubble had been cleared away from the square. Miraculously, only six lives had been lost. The bodies of the dead lay wrapped in makeshift shrouds near the city's walls. Someone had unobtrusively taken care of the survivors, since the streets were clear of the wandering homeless.

It was nearly twilight. Remo and Chiun had worked with the Mayans for nearly eighteen hours salvaging what they could of the city. Several of the men had collapsed from exhaustion. Po, the improvised bandages on his legs blackened from soot, slept in the open courtyard as Nata-Ah rummaged through the vacant buildings for a new dressing for his wound.

"The boy served us well," Chiun said.

"Yeah, he worked out okay after that stunt in the palace. I guess I won't spank the little bugger."

Chiun surveyed the area with his alert hazel eyes. "The damage is not so great as I feared."

Remo shrugged. "Nothing a good team of masons couldn't fix in a decade or two." He laughed. He was bone-tired, but he knew he couldn't rest until he had delivered the bad news he'd put off for most of the day.

"I might as well tell you, Lizzie's gone," he blurted.

"That is too much to hope for," Chiun said.

"It's true. She took off in the time module. I don't think we'll see her again."

"I do," Chiun said disgustedly. "That woman is like misfortune. She always turns up when you need her least."

"Well, she's not going to turn up now."

Chiun pointed, his face forming an expression of distaste. "Think again, o brilliant one."

Walking from the crumbled city wall, her shirt torn at the shoulder, her hair turned gray-black from dirt and plaster dust, Lizzie ambled over to them and sat down in the dust without a word.

"Where'd you come from?" Remo asked.

"Outside the city. I've been finding temporary homes for the villagers. It's no bed of roses out there, either, but the damage isn't as bad as it is here." Resting on her elbows, she closed her eyes and threw her head back in fatigue.

"So that's where the villagers went," Remo said.

"*She* helped?" Chiun asked incredulously.

"I know it's not my style," Lizzie said, a bitter smile playing around her mouth.

"What about the pod? Did you try it?"

"Oh, yes. It worked. I sent a vase up in it as an experiment. Turned the switch, presto. Vase gone." She looked into the distance. "I put a note in it. I thought maybe Dick Diehl would come exploring the temple some day and find it."

"Hey, wait a minute. A vase? What about you? I thought you were going home."

She chuckled, a half-laugh born of deep exhaustion. "Yeah, I did, too. And then I started to think about you here, and about all these slobs in trouble, and about Cooligan and how he felt good even though he knew he was going to die here. . . . Oh, I don't know," she said, getting wearily to her feet. "It was a hell of a time to develop a conscience."

Remo took her hand. "Thanks for sticking around," he said.

"Think nothing—" Her hands flailed in the air and she fell, sprawling. "What was *that*?"

The earth moved again. "Another tremor," Chiun said. "Milder. This time will be easier."

The boy scrambled to his feet along with the sleepy Mayans, who blinked in astonishment at the new rumblings.

"Another chance," Lizzie said, almost in a whisper. "I can't believe it. I never thought . . ." Her words drifted off as her eyes met Remo's. "Do you want to stay? I'll stay if you do."

"I don't think we have to this time," Remo said, watching her eyes flood with relief. "Will the time module work?"

"Your guess is as good as mine," she said, running for the Temple of Magic. "I sent the vase into the future, and then set the controls back, but the vase didn't return."

Remo stopped in his tracks. "It didn't?"

"No," Lizzie said quietly.

"Something's wrong. I don't know if we ought to risk it."

"It is time to risk something," Chiun said, his hand on Po's shoulder. "I have spent quite enough time in this place, and I wish to return. I will go."

"If you go, I'll go," Remo said.

"Well, nobody's going without me," Lizzie laughed as she tried to keep her balance on the shifting earth.

"Okay, everybody in," Remo commanded, when they reached the temple. "Might as well give this thing another try." He helped Lizzie into the pod. Imperiously, Chiun followed her in.

"You too, squirt," Remo said to the boy.

Po looked over his shoulder. Footsteps were approaching. Nata-Ah appeared, holding a length of cotton bandage in her hands. Her face fell at the sight of the new gods preparing to depart.

"I cannot go," the boy said awkwardly. "Someone must remain to rebuild the city—"

"For God's sake, that'll take years," Remo said.

"I have years," the boy said quietly. "I have my whole life."

"Now, I can't let you—"

"Please," Po said. "I belong here now, as I never belonged in my own time. I have come to the end of my journey. As my father predicted, I have walked with the gods, and spoken for them. Now it is time for the gods to go. Let them leave behind their voice."

He limped to the doorway of the time module and bowed to Chiun. Nata-Ah was behind him.

Chiun rose, walked over to the two children, and whispered something in Po's ear. The boy nodded. Then they both bowed to Chiun and to Remo and to Lizzie with the cool authority of born rulers.

"Please enter," the boy said to Remo in a voice that sounded more like a man's than a boy's.

Remo went in.

With another bow, Po closed the door and threw the switch. "Good-bye, my friends," he called.

Chapter Sixteen

Lizzie came to in despair. "The log," she moaned. "I forgot the damned captain's log."

"Not so fast. We may still be there," Remo said. He opened the door.

The Temple of Magic was in ruins. Outside the door to the pod lay a freshly broken vase. "Look here," Remo said, picking up the pieces. "It must have rolled out of the pod. I think we made it."

Among the shards of pottery was a small scrap of parchment, grown as fragile as an insect's wings with the years. On it was a faint message: "I love you, Dick."

Remo handed the parchment to Lizzie. "Is this all you were going to tell him?"

She smiled. "In the end, that was all there was to say."

In the outer chamber, Remo found the ancient laser weapon he had saved to take to Smith. "Everything's just the way we left it."

"Is it?" Chiun said, beckoning them back to the wreckage of the plane. In the chamber reserved for the gods' flaming chariot was a blank space. The *Cassandra* and everything in her was gone.

"But—we just came from there," Remo said.

Chiun held up a precautionary finger. "You forget, we left five thousand years ago. And five thousand years ago was this machine destroyed."

"Who did it?" Lizzie demanded hotly. "Who would have done such a thing?"

"The only sensible one among you. The boy. It was my last request to him before we left."

Remo stared at him in astonishment. "Do you know what you did? What's been lost?"

"What has been lost? The opportunity for others to walk yet again in the footsteps of Kukulcan, bringing their modern ways to an ancient world? Oh, they would come with good intentions, these others, just as we did. And like ourselves, they would bring confusion and violence to their land. No, Remo. It is a mistake to inflict our time on another. We have left Po as our ambassador. Trust him."

They walked outside. The overgrown jungle was back to replace the village square of Yaxbenhaltun.

You will be as dust in the wind of the sea, Remo remembered. Quintanodan's prophecy had come true; the splendor of the Maya was no more. "Do you think the Olmec won, after all? Are they still around, calling themselves the Lost Tribes?"

"We'll never know," Lizzie said. She tramped through the high grass to the east of the temple. "There's no volcano," she said. "Bocatan's gone." Something on the ground fixed her attention. "Remo, look here."

A mound of blackened, moss-covered rock protruded from the earth beside her. "This wasn't here before."

"It's just a rock."

"No," she said excitedly, scratching at the moss with her fingernails. "That's *stone.* Cut stone. This was built." Her eyes flashed. "Another temple, maybe. Or, better yet, a tomb. Maybe the city was reorganized after the earthquake. Oh, God, I've got to get a team together."

"How about your friend Dick Diehl?" Remo suggested. "He might be interested."

"He might," Lizzie said. "Think I could go with you as far as the first town with a telephone?"

"If you must," Chiun said.

Lizzie looked up at the old man. He was smiling.

"What am I going to tell Smitty?" Remo lamented as he and Chiun walked through the double doors of Folcroft Sanitarium. Under Remo's arm was a box marked "Fragile," which had flown with them from Guatemala City.

"Tell him the truth."

"But there's no evidence anymore. The plane's gone, the time module's gone, even Cooligan's log is gone."

Chiun tapped the box. "You have the gun."

"Yeah. And the flowers. I brought some of the white flowers."

Smith opened the box and sifted through a pile of greenish metallic powder covering some rotting greens. "What is this supposed to be?"

Remo looked inside. The weapon had disintegrated during the flight. "It used to be a laser gun," Remo said, feeling foolish as he spoke. "We found them, just the way Dr. Diehl described . . ."

"This isn't funny, Remo," Smith said acidly. "Now, I realize that you may have cause to feel angry, but this sort of practical joke goes far beyond the limits of good taste. This could have been a matter of national security, and I'm sure that when you're calm you'll realize that not every assignment turns out to be terribly interesting. Nevertheless—"

"Hold it, hold it," Remo said. "Not interesting?"

"I'm referring to Dr. Diehl, of course. I did try to reach you as soon as I found out this morning, but by then you were already en route back from Guatemala. There was nothing I could do."

"What about Dr. Diehl?"

"He's changed his story. Practically admits he was lying. 'Strain,' he calls it. Now that he's no longer suffering under this so-called strain, he's confessed to a certain confusion about the lasers he thought he saw. The CIA is convinced that they never existed. So am I. Just some hostile Indians, no doubt."

"What about the Red Cross transmissions?"

"Garbled. They were probably panicking because of the impending crash of their helicopter. We've sent in rescue squads for the bodies. Your work, I suppose, excavating them from the wreckage?"

"All but Elizabeth Drake. She was alive."

"So I've heard. The rescue team looked for the two of you for some time. Where did you go, by the way?"

"Oh—"

"We continued on our training expedition," Chiun chimed in. "The jungle was ideal for our purposes, o illustrious Emperor."

"That's good," Smith said absently. He was leafing through the most recent batch of computer printouts on his desk. "Er—anything else?"

"I guess not," Remo said.

"Then leave. You're not even supposed to be here at the sanitarium," Smith said.

"He thought that laser weapon was a *joke*," Remo fumed as they headed toward Folcroft's front entrance.

"It did look more like a joke than a gun," Chiun said, chuckling. "Besides, emperors usually discard the truth. Otherwise, politics would be impossible to understand."

A sweating man rushing into the sanitarium whizzed by, narrowly missing a head-on collision with Remo.

"Hey, watch it, fella."

"'Scuse me," the man said, smiling twitchily. "I was in kind of a rush there."

"It is quite all right," Chiun said graciously.

The man appraised the frail-looking old Oriental in his yellow gown. "Say, I know you two."

"No, you don't," Remo said.

"Sure. Don't you remember?"

"Let's get out of here," Remo whispered in Korean. As it was, they had left too many witnesses through the years. Remo was not supposed to exist. For him to be recognized was unthinkable.

"No, really," the man insisted. "It was out at Edwards Air Base. I ejected from a burning F-24 and got a streamer for a chute. You saved my life."

"Oh," Remo said, forcing a casual smile. "Well, just forget that, okay?" He backed away.

"That's what you said before. But I'll tell you, if it wasn't for you, I'd have never gotten to see my kid. Oh, here." He fumbled in his pockets for two cigars and thrust them at Remo and Chiun.

"It's a boy," he said proudly. "I'm just coming to tell my pop he's a grandpop. He's a patient here."

"That was thoughtful," Chiun said.

"Nah. When they got empty planes over at the base, we can use them, long as none of the brass finds out." He laughed. "Hey, you got kids?"

Remo shook his head.

"It's the greatest feeling in the world. I feel like it's the first time old Mike Cooligan ever did anything just exactly right. Man, this baby is a born flyer."

"Cooligan?" Remo repeated.

"Yeah. Irish from way back. My pop's name is Kurt. That's what we've named the kid. Kurt Cooligan, after his grandpop. The old man's going to love that."

"Kurt Cooligan," Remo whispered, choking on the sounds. "Going to be a pilot too, huh?" He smiled weakly.

"The best. I tell you, this kid's going to know all the basics of every fighter ever made by the time he's twelve. He's going to go to military school, and then a good college, Harvard, maybe, so he gets every chance I never got. Hell, with Harvard he could be president if he wants to. An astronaut, even. Geez, listen to me foam at the mouth. The kid's not even a week old." He laughed and slapped Remo's back heartily.

"Uh, I dunno," Remo ventured. "Maybe flying wouldn't be such a good idea . . ."

Chiun elbowed him hard in the ribs.

"Oof." Remo doubled over.

"My associate means to say that we congratulate you on your good fortune but, alas, we must take our leave."

"Sure," Cooligan said. "Say, is your friend all right?" He gestured to Remo, who was trying to refill the oxygen supply that had so suddenly left his lungs.

"It is nothing," Chiun assured him.

* * *

"Would you mind giving me a little warning next time?" Remo complained once they were off the Folcroft grounds. "I don't know why you always take me by surprise."

"Because you are a trusting and foolish white man," Chiun gloated.

"I mean why you'd want to," Remo objected.

"That is because your mouth usually contains more material than your brain."

"Just because I told that nut—"

"Fortunately, you told that nut nothing. If, by chance, your words had succeeded in dissuading Mr. Mike Cooligan from forcing his son to be a pilot, the history of the world might be changed."

"So what?" Remo said. "I've been hearing this history-of-the-world crap until it's coming out my gazoo. I don't care about history. I read Cooligan's diary. That poor guy gave up his life for some dumb Air Force mission that never even happened."

"I too read the diary," Chiun said. "Kurt Cooligan did not give his life for a mission, but for a world. And that world was better for him. Does that not make his life worthy in your eyes?"

"Kukulcan," Remo said. "I guess it's something to become a god."

Chiun grunted. "If one cannot be the Master of Sinanju, it is acceptable," he said.

"It's funny, thinking of Cooligan the way he was in the captain's log, and knowing that right now he's just a baby."

"It is as the Mayans say. The past and the future are one."

"But that doesn't make sense," Remo said. "I mean, if that were true, you'd be able to read my future, right?"

"Oh, but I can, I can," Chiun said mysteriously.

"You can?"

"Yes. In your future is a long training expedition."

"A *what*? We just came off one of those."

"You were inadequate. We will have to begin anew."

"Oh, no," Remo said. "No more North Pole. No more desert. No jungle, no, sir."

"You see? You know the details already. You are a born prophet, my son. Which way is north?"

"That way. Toward the motel. I've got eight quarters for your vibrating bed. And I'll send out for room service."

Chiun's eyes narrowed. "Duck à l'orange?"

"I'll kill the duck myself if I have to," Remo said.

"Cable TV?"

"All night long."

"A swimming pool, perhaps?"

"Kidney shaped."

Chiun put his bony arm around Remo. "Ah, well, there is time for the training expedition tomorrow, I suppose. Would you like me to recite one of the Ung poems of the great Wang? It is very short, only six hundred stanzas."

Remo swallowed. "Love it," he said.

The old man beamed. "Sometimes, Remo, you are not so bad for a white boy."

Epilogue

LOS ANGELES TIMES
PROGRESSO, GUATEMALA (API)

The husband and wife team of Elizabeth and Richard Diehl, both archaeologists at UCLA, have unearthed what could prove to be the oldest intact tomb in the western world.

Dating from the third millennium, B.C., it is the tomb of one of the first kings of the Classical Period in ancient Mayan civilization.

Named simply Po, the occupant of the tomb was known as the Lame King. According to the inscriptions on his sarcophagus, King Po did so much to make the Mayan empire the advanced society we regard it today that he was called "the voice of the gods" by his people. Next to the king's remains was uncovered the sarcophagus of his only wife, the beautiful and just Queen Nata-Ah.

Lining the walls of the tomb were many precious artifacts and sculptures, including a magnificent redition of the famous white god Kukulcan, adorned with the traditional serpents and feathers found on other statues of the Mayan deity.

Two other statues, also found in the tomb, are currently causing lively speculation in archaeological circles. Previously unidentified in Mayan findings, the statues depict two human males. One is an old man of obviously Oriental features. The other is younger, possibly a warrior. The features of the statue are unimpressive except for a pair of exceptionally thick wrists.

CHIUN'S OWN BOOK

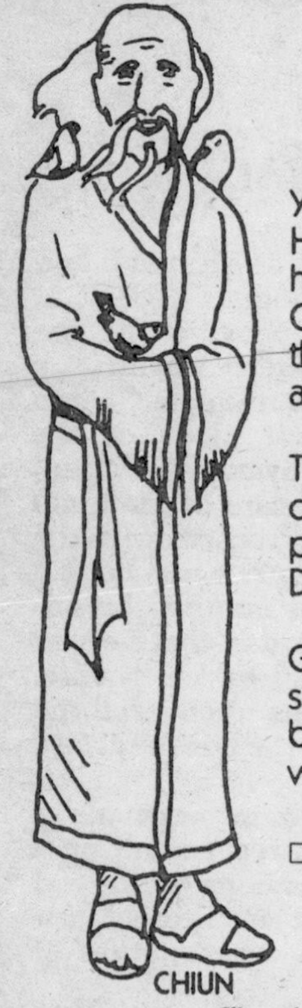

Want to know more about Chiun and the House of Sinanju?

You can find it all in THE ASSASSIN'S HANDBOOK. Everything. From the history of the House of Sinanju and Chiun's almost-favorite Ung poem to the Assassin's Quick Weight Loss Diet and 37 Steps to Sexual Ecstasy.

THE ASSASSIN'S HANDBOOK also contains an original, never-before published DESTROYER novella: "The Day Remo Died".

Get this one-of-a-kind, hardcover-size trade paperback at your local bookstore, or order it from Pinnacle with the coupon below.

☐ 41-847-7 THE ASSASSIN'S HANDBOOK
$6.95 created by
RICHARD SAPIR and WARREN MURPHY
compiled and edited by Will Murray

Clip and mail this page with your order

PINNACLE BOOKS, INC.—Reader Service Dept.
1430 Broadway, New York, NY 10018

Please send me the book(s) I have checked above. I am enclosing $_______ (please add 75¢ to cover postage and handling). Send check or money order only—no cash or C.O.D.'s.

Mr./Mrs./Miss ____________________

Address ____________________

City ____________________ State/Zip ____________________

Please allow six weeks for delivery. Prices subject to change without notice.